CIRCUS ✚ THE SKIN

April —

Thanks so much for buying a book! Hope you enjoy, cousin!

Keith McClary

Circus + The Skin
© 2018 by Keith McCleary
Edited by George Cotronis
Book Design by George Cotronis
http://cotronis.com/

Interior Art by Ken Knudtsen
https://www.kenknudtsen.com/

Portions of this book have previously appeared in Weave Magazine and New Dead Families.

Kraken Press
Please visit us on the web at www.krakenpress.com
ISBN: 978-91-979725-2-9

No portion of this book may be reproduced by any means, mechanical, electronic, or otherwise, without first obtaining the permission of the copyright holder.

PRAISE FOR CIRCUS + THE SKIN

"Keith McCleary writes like a hard-boiled Nick Cave, while the wandering spirits of Harry Crews and Katherine Dunn look on in grim whimsy. McCleary's face-paced yet character-driven tale of geeks and lion-tamers, bendable women and sinister showmen, and an illustrated man named Sue who can never outrun his past—or his present—never flags. CIRCUS+THE SKIN is a high-wire act of the tender, the fierce, and the deeply macabre."

—Adrian Van Young, author of *Shadows in Summerland* and *The Man Who Noticed Everything*.

"Unflinching and lyrical tale of a circus at the end of an era and an illustrated man whose tattoos whisper beneath his skin. McCleary's prose is as a fever dream told by Ray Bradbury to Cormac McCarthy—a love letter in blood and ink mapping our collective journey from Vietnam to Coney Island toward an American doom from which escape is just another word for nothing left to lose. An impressive and unsettling debut."

—JS Breukelaar, author of *Aletheia* and *American Monster*.

"Step right up and take a gander at one of the strangest circus acts ever assembled. Keith McCleary writes with the brutality of a sledgehammer and the precision of a high-wire artist. The America he conjures up in this unforgettable carny noir is old and riddled with darkness. With style for days and prose that sings on the page, CIRCUS+THE SKIN is a show you don't want to miss."

—Jim Ruland, author of *Forest of Fortune*

"In the shadow of Ray Bradbury's *The Illustrated Man*, Keith McCleary has sketched his own unique dark imagery with CIRCUS+THE SKIN. A circus without heart would just be an accident on the side of the road—nothing but gawking, fear, and a momentary spectacle. But this novel does much more than that. Filled with passion, death, mystery, and wonder, this is a powerful tale that sprinkles horror, noir, and the grotesque onto a sideshow of the transgressive, creating an original, satisfying journey."

—Richard Thomas, author of Thriller-nominee *Breaker*.

"When his flesh twitched, the tiny mouths flickered, the tiny green-and-gold eyes winked, the tiny pink hands gestured. There were yellow meadows and blue rivers and mountains and stars and suns and planets spread in a Milky Way across his chest. The people themselves were in twenty or more odd groups upon his arms, shoulders, back, sides, and wrists, as well as on the flat of his stomach. You found them in forests of hair, lurking among a constellation of freckles, or peering from armpit caverns, diamond eyes aglitter. Each seemed intent upon his own activity, each was a separate gallery portrait."

-Ray Bradbury, *The Illustrated Man*

tattoo
ART & CIRCUS
SHOW
MUTANT
FEB 6
"ADMISSION
IS FREE
YOUR MONEY
WORTHLESS TO
BUT WE
TAKE YOUR
KNUDTSE

PART 1
JUNE 22-23, 1983
ROOMS

"We told you we had living, breathing monstrosities. You laughed at them, shuddered at them. And, yet, but for the accident of birth, you might be one as they are."

- Carnival Barker, *Freaks*

THE LONG WALK.
ONE.
I want you to know I ain't a natural freak like some. I bought and paid for every bit of ink on me, in all manner of ways. But I don't think on those times no more.

The morning had risen gray, with crows crying in the nearby trees. They bawled like children and made me think of you. The air smelled like puke and looked like it. The circus had been traveling to a burg south of Pickinpaw, but of course we'd got there first.

The rest of our caravan was trapped in mud on route 20 or 40 or whatever it was coming up from the south. It was hard to remember there were other roads, other places. Out there past the wheat field the world rolled into summer—late June, nineteen eighty-three in the year of our Lord. But here in the low country, time crawled slow. Here it was only locust season, and the locusts had been high as we'd driven north the day before, their guts plastering to our windshield. Here it seemed there was only one road, leading only to one place, to a mud-gutted highway with crows crying in the trees, and the air still and rank and cool.

Omar had woken first, along with Cook, and they groused each other over while beans steamed in a rusty kettle they'd found in the freak truck. It was lucky we had that, I supposed.

Cook had shacked up drunk with us the night before, but food—real food—was back with the rest of the trucks. I guessed those lovely French tumblers who cooked better than Cook were right then breaking out the fixings for crêpes or French toast or Belgian waffles or some other foreign sweet-smelling thing.

We had beans. Cook had found one can wedged into a camp kitchen the Simple Twins had been trying to open with their teeth. It was roughly a gallon-size, with an expiration date from around the Civil War. Cook cracked the lid and it didn't smell any worse than the breeze, and he'd found the kettle too and started a fire. Then he lit a cigar to cover the stink from the beans and the air.

Omar watched the highway and hills. He was the strongman, and the breeze blew around him and he didn't flinch. Winds whipped the little hairs on his arms and beard and head. I watched him from the stoop of the truck while I rolled a cigarette, happy to sit for a while in my ink with no stares.

My ink was happy too. I felt the tattoos buzzing in the weak dawn sun, watched them crawl on my arms and grin at me.

Etta sat nearby, leftover like Cook from the wrong truck the night before. She was one of the Russian riders but she was still all right. She could do flips on and off horses, and you might think that would have busted her up beneath, but I saw no problem there. Everyone said the ringmaster was half-queer anyway. He kept Etta on his arm like a trained bird, whenever she wasn't jumping on or off some horse.

Me and Etta didn't talk much, and when we did it was a few words only, so as not to clutter the space when we lay side by side. The nights she stayed with me were always good, and some mornings were good too. But others were cold and strange. This morning Etta had woke up second, got the Twins cleaned and shitted, found them some spoons to play with, gathered branches for our fire, then sat down on the stoop while we waited for beans.

Etta had a small journal with her, scrawled with notes I couldn't figure. As the fire dipped and waned, she ripped pages from the journal to stoke the flames. I wondered what the pages were, and hoped they didn't mean much.

So it was me, and Omar, and Etta, and Cook, and the Simple Twins under skies ready to tear apart like wet paper. I was watching Etta and the way she kept tucking her hair behind her ears when a shadow came over the farthest hill.

Omar called out the obvious—that some man was coming, some thin man, some thin man with a hat, some thin man with a hat and a suitcase—over and over in his eastern European shout, each time adding one detail like we had no eyes to see the man ourselves. Cook grunted he wasn't feeding nobody extra, and Etta whispered something to me about him being extra and made me laugh all right. We waited for Mr. Tall Suitcased Stringbones to walk the highway from there to here.

We saw his grin before we could make out his face. He had big lips that pulled back over big teeth when he smiled, and he was in a violet suit with a matching top hat. I'd seen a lot of getups almost like his, but never on someone walking down a road just past dawn, on his own with nothing but a suitcase. "Ahoy there!" the man called. "Have you lost your friends?"

"What?" Omar called back.

"I say," the man said as he got close, "Your truck looks lonely. You missing some people? I saw some other trucks like yours when I was walking."

"Doubtful," said Cook. "We got others, but they're farther'n' you could've walked."

"Is that so," the man said, not asking but saying, and his smile held as he looked at me. "Beautiful," he said, to my skin.

I hadn't gotten that before. I sat and smoked at him.

"Sue's a pretty one, all right," Cook said, sneering. The man cocked his head.

"Sue?" he said. "That what they call you?"

His eyes scanned the side of the trailer behind me. He found my name and the painting of me showing off my tats, squeezed in between Omar juggling barbells and the bearded lady—wherever she was. He read the words under my name aloud.

"TATTOO SUE," he said. "Got a ring to it anyway." He looked the trailer all over again. "These murals are spectacular. Hell, you all are real old-time circus. Feels like I stepped back a hundred years."

"I ain't got no extra," said Cook then, looking at the meager helping of beans in our pot, like a question had been asked. The stranger followed Cook's finger, then seemed to shake his head once to clear it.

"That's fine," the man said. "I seek the town yonder." He smiled bigger. "I'm sure I'll see you again."

And he kept walking, and we watched him until he disappeared over the horizon.

"Don't know how he thinks we'll see him twice," Cook said.

"Maybe he know someone we know," said Etta.

"Well," said Cook, "he dresses like it anyways."

Etta went back to reading, but her face looked different. The morning mist was burning off in the grip of dirty sky. I felt for some reason that I was waiting for something, or maybe it was just Etta looking strange. I leaned back on the stoop, rolled another cigarette, and lost track of time awhile.

TWO.

The violet-suited man was the highlight of things for a few hours at least, as the sky turned from gray to orange then blue, hanging over us in that muddy field next to a dead forest. The air warmed and the air had begun to buzz. Locusts clustered on reeds and anywhere else they found room.

By 10 o'clock my brain was crawling. Circus rules when trucks got split was you waited for the last ones to catch up before moving on. Our truck had been moving fastest, so here we sat. The Twins were somewhere playing and Etta had gone inside, so it was Cook and Omar and me. I smoked till I realized I'd run out of tobacco if I kept going, and while I assumed Pickinpaw had a smoke shop I knew not to risk it in these highway backwaters. I put my stick out on my knuckles and sat up on the stoop.

I was thinking about that empty highway with no trucks on it. I wondered if we were really south of Pickinpaw, or if we'd got lost on a sideroad in last night's rain. I started to feel like when I was young, soldiering and waiting for the boats to pick us up from some nameless island.

Omar kept pacing and staring off down the highway, and when Cook made some comment that it wouldn't make the other trucks come no quicker, Omar smacked him to the ground.

Cook got up and cursed that Omar owed him a replacement cigar, then went off behind the truck to have a smoke and a nip in peace.

All of Omar's pacing was making me anxious too. There was a sycamore sapling at the edge of our makeshift camp that had been giving me supple shakes of its leaves all morning, just begging to be a bullseye.

I decided to engage Omar in a game of Throwin' a Knife at a Tree. So. Knife. Tree. I went into the freak truck and hauled my Bowie out of my rucksack, then wandered back outside.

Omar stamped over to me by the third time the blade dug into the bark.

"What noise you makin'? What you doing?" he demanded.

"Just passin' time," I said. I handed him the knife by its hilt, and he looked at it at like he had to decide whether to eat it or to cave it in my head. The moment slid past us, and Omar threw that knife fit to split the sycamore in two.

"Good one," I said, and that got us started.

We'd only been throwing a half hour, talking about traveling north or where the other trucks were or where was good eating in the places we'd lived, when another storm started rolling in. Cook saw it first, and called out a curse while he brought in his supplies. I grabbed my Bowie and helped Omar shutter the windows on the freak truck, and Etta held the door for us as we ran in.

Inside we lit the lamps, then realized we hadn't seen the Simple Twins since after breakfast.

"Shit," I said.

Omar and Cook's faces said they didn't give a rat. Etta was already at the door, waiting for me. We headed back outside into the storm and dark.

THREE.

The wind was loud and fast and sucked the words out of our mouths. It had come up quick as a twister, although I knew it wasn't so. The winds spit grass and dust across our eyes, and insects got caught up in gusts before they could fly away. Out to the horizon I could see the trees torn one way and another, so whatever it was we were getting the ass-end of was spread out across as many acres as I could count.

Etta and I headed into the woods back to back, covering the trees without losing sight of each other. And we called for the Twins—me for Ben and her for Tom, just to keep it easy.

We found a raccoon with its brains dashed against the low spines of a pine tree, left there by storms or predators. The bracken densened as we ventured farther from the truck, giving way as we pushed through. I flashed to one hoary thicket or another from the wars of my youth, all pushed together here and made gray with muted tones, emptied of the rotted greens and browns of those hot days gone.

Now this is something I don't talk about, but my skin itches some. I had my palms read by a gypsy when I was discharged, and she saw strangeness in the patterns on my skin. Over a bottle of vermouth she told me most of what she did was hoodoo, but occasional she got a glimpse of something bigger.

She said one of them times was looking at my tattoos.

Though my inks were nothing special, knives and hearts and roses and snakes and skulls, and though they'd been done at different times, in different cities, by different men, the gypsy said they formed patterns she recognized, like a map in my flesh. She said she wouldn't be surprised if they called to me in the soft hours and little darknesses.

I would not presume to say, even if I wore whisper-skin, that larger forces had ever demonstrated much concern with me. It's just that sometimes my skin itched, like fingers at a dog's collar. It itched me now, through downed trees and brush.

Etta reached behind to lock elbows, like we weren't a rider and a tattooed man, but twin acrobats instead. I spoke to her in my rusty tongue and Etta to me in Russian verse. Winds ripped trees and bark apart, and we stood and huddled close till we could move again.

We found Simple Tom first, alone and crying, naked and clinging to a torn-up tree so hard Etta had to smack him loose. I grabbed him from behind and got him in a hold, so he walked where I walked him. Simple Ben was just nearby inside a hollowed trunk. The two boys saw one another, and wailed into each other's faces.

I grabbed Ben's naked hide and walked a few more steps before the light from the freak truck peered at us through the trees. A hundred more steps, a hundred fifty, and we were out. Above us now the storm was cooling, getting ready to go again.

Behind the last bout of rain a blackness lingered, though it couldn't have been more than late afternoon. The sky was the color of river mud, and no light shown.

We made it to the truck and pushed the twins inside, smelling something resembling food but was probably just beans.

FOUR.
A single candle hung an amber light on the truck's insides. Cook and Omar played cards away from the windows, with tensed shoulders. They looked up as we came in hauling naked simpletons.

"You got 'em, at least," said Cook. Departing thunder echoed. "'Spose that's good."

"Good enough nothin' you useless shit," I almost said, but instead I grabbed a towel from the camp kitchen, and another from a wash basin beneath the bunks. Etta wrapped Tom and Ben, and I scooped them two scoops of crusted beans from the pot.

"Them shits share one serving," snarled Cook. "We don't need fat retards." He grabbed Tom's bowl from him and Tom cried out.

I stood and snatched Tom's bowl from Cook. Cook yelped. I threw the bowl down in front of the Twins. They stared up at me.

I glared back at them and shouted "Eat up!"

They started crying like a choir, and dragged their food to the other end of the cabin.

I sat down. Etta was looking at me. I didn't look back.

Still looking she said, "Others not coming. We should go

soon. Find town."

I ticked open a shutter. Outside, the wind was quieting.

"Yeah, all right," I said. "If that purple-suited fella could do it. Sure."

"I did not like his face," said Omar softly. One eye glinted in the dark.

I hadn't liked it neither, nor nothing else in the purple man's whole body, but I thought I might eat my own skin if I sat in that shack a second longer.

Cook dragged himself up. The open window cast a low glare on one side of his face, while the candle lent a glow to the other. He spat something black on the floor and stared at me.

"One of us should stay while the others go," said Cook. "On lookout."

"I will stay," said Omar.

"Ayuh. We'll stay," said Cook, and sat back in his chair.

"Fine," I said, and looked at Etta, who hadn't stopped looking at me. She wiped her mouth and stood up from the table, and I followed her to the door.

"Keep a light burning," I said, and walked out. Cook and Omar's eyes seared holes in the back of my head.

Outside the trailer Etta stretched and then I did. As the door shut behind us I looked back on the Twins, eating their beans. Etta watched them too. The sky was brighter, but clouds trailed over us like grief.

I thought to turn then to Etta and apologize for the knockups inside the trailer, but I didn't have words. I thought to suggest we take just the cab and the Twins ourselves and drive to town, leaving Cook and Omar to freeze their asses in this sorry field.

I turned to Etta to say it, when a second figure came up the highway.

The figure was skewed and flattened, twisted and limping as it came. I pointed, and Etta cocked her head and then walked slowly toward it, and then she was running and calling out.

When I came back from my last tour I lived in New York a time, working the show on Coney Island. There was a girl about ten years old who lived there. She had a camera and cased the boardwalk, taking photographs for five cents apiece. She came around my booth nights, and we'd mosey together on the beach. I'd give her nickels and tell her to photograph what she chose. She snapped birds and sea and stones, garbage and the crowds, but she liked the dog races most. She'd come to my booth on Sunday evenings to show me how she froze the dogs in flight.

I'd close my eyes and listen to her laugh, and in her laugh I'd see you.

Now, as Etta sprinted up that muddy road, it was the racing hounds I thought of, all supple limbs and skin.

But there was nothing beautiful when that thing in the road started to scream.

FIVE.

Her limbs were tied in corded ropes that chewed her skin and she'd been folded over, walking with her wrists by her ankles. It was a posture might tear a regular man apart.

But she was Mei Shen, the Rubber Woman. Getting folded, she could take.

Still she cried as we untied her, she'd been in knots so long. I had to go in on the ropes with my Bowie, breathing slow as the blade worked the twine.

After she was loose she lay unstretched while Etta sat with her, brushing bracken from her hair. The commotion brought out Cook and Omar, and the bean-fed Simple Twins crossed that flat wet grass to see what had been drug up. Cook offered his flask, which Mei Shen refused. Etta offered water, which she took.

"We can carry you into the trailer," I said.

"One minute," Mei Shen said. "Let me lie."

In a minute she began to talk.

Mei Shen had woken up with pigs and rain.

She'd come to and felt horrendous hurt, her body twisted fit to snap, and then she heard boars. Opening her eyes showed her she was ass-up in a drainage ditch off a side road. Mei Shen couldn't make sense of how she got there. The last thing she remembered was rolling along in the tumbler's truck with a lightning storm outside the trailer.

But now she saw a sounder of boars huddled nearby, digging for mushrooms under the cover of firs. The moment held as her limbs found themselves in the mud.

Then she watched as one hog looked up at sky and squawked. The others followed suit, before running into the forest.

And the sky opened.

The downpour where we'd lost the Twins had almost drowned Mei Shen. The ditch started filling fast and she hoisted herself up before rainwater got in her lungs. She knew she'd been hog-tied, and she smelled oil. Working every contortionist trick, she crawled up the embankment slick with slop and dragged herself to the road.

Mei Shen had been in a caravan with the acrobats and horse trainers—several trucks with a lot of folk and animals besides. Now it was a plume of smoke against the sky, the yellow caravans licked clean of paint as they burned.

She saw a pair of white horses tied at the snout, running into the trees to escape the rain. Each fought for control from the other, yanking and pulling sideways as they went. The field had turned to wet clay, and the air sucked up light in raindrops. The horses only saw her a moment, then pulled at each other again. She took one lurching step toward them and they fell back into the trees.

Then she saw something near her, ashen and smoking, black and red, a lump of charcoal in the grass. It had hands and teeth, and little fingers.

The fingers stretched toward her.

Mei Shen started screaming then, falling and walking and falling through the storm, a blur of mud and sky.

Etta sat over her now, shushing and calming, Cook whispering "shit" and Omar pacing, glaring at me like throttling my neck could make it right.

Inside me things turned over. I was on my first tour, and I

was young. I was talking to this old Crow Indian named Jack, who'd been working infantry some time longer than me. It was our night watch, and the trees around us crawled with dead zipperheads whose faces were tore up with the scattershot I'd sent through them.

I was drunk then always, and told Jack about the faces in the dark. He nodded, and told me he saw them too. The quiet stretched and I asked Jack how a fellow dealt with it, all them years a soldier.

Jack looked at me blank and just said, "Don't." And he went to sleep, leaving me up alone.

Sitting in that jungle I had felt space open. Wind blew through the trees and the insects and the peepers rose. I felt a presence just past the long grasses. In the light of the swamp something glittered and shone.

As I watched, an eye had opened in the darkness. It hung in shadow and looked at me unblinking. It was as if it had always been there.

The eye looked through my heart open like a house, I by its entrance, keeping my secrets there like they had any worth. Beyond the entrance of my heart the eye saw shadows, back rooms, empty and covered with the dust of time.

I'd come to later in the night, feeling strange and oddly calm. The fear in me had gotten stored away. In my mind I saw doors closed down the ends of long hallways, doors holding back the loathesome bits of me.

There are rooms in me, I'd thought then. And while Jack slept and I kept watch for my platoon in the blue marshes far from home, I found some kind of peace.

But I know now the price for storing shadows. I know how hard they are to clear out, once they're in. I know what you become if your soul's a house of long hallways and rooms you can't get into.

I looked down at Mei Shen's broken body, smelling as the blood rose off her. I felt a key open a door for peeling fear.

SIX.

"Let's take the truck and get the hell outta here," I said.

"The others might be lookin' for us," said Cook. "We'll be hard to find if we're movin' all around."

The group glared at him.

"Or we might just leave a note on a tree," he said. We propped a bright piece of wood against a maple with words smeared across it in grease.

Omar laid Mei on a cot in the back of the trailer, and made fists at the Simple Twins when they came near her. Etta slid in the cab with the ring of keys and started the rig. I hopped in shotgun with Cook behind me. The truck woke up with a wet, grinding retch and Etta aimed south, where clouds crawled from the corners of the sky.

Everywhere the air was still. Etta drove slow, the rumble of the motor cutting through quiet. Cook peeked through the window with suspicion, like this weren't just a road and cornfields but some unholy place.

I thought on the tiny hand Mei Shen had found, and what became of the body it was attached to. I wondered if we'd all died, and if this was the land of the dead.

As we drove, we saw tent canopies hanging from the trees. They were yellow and red with circles and other shapes, crosshatched now with tears and dirt, draped across the skeleton branches of elms and sycamores blown clean of leaves in the overlapping storms. They hung along the tree line between the roads and the fields like dried skins. There were the tents for the sideshows, for the midway, for our freakshow. The ropes that bound them dripped down through the trees and dragged like veins across the grass. Some stretched across the road, and the truck thumped each one that we ran over.

Etta leaned forward in her seat. "The mud will be too thick," she said, and pointed down the road where the way got slick. She rolled to a stop.

"Can't walk," said Omar, pointing to Mei Shen.

"I walk," said Mei Shen. She got halfway off the cot then sucked in her breath, and Omar made her lay back.

I opened the truck door and got out, then took a few paces down the road before coming back.

"I think Mei's trailer is up ahead," I said to Etta. "But the fire got put out by the storm. Just a black mess now."

Etta pulled off to park under a thick grove of trees. No one wanted to sit in the truck anymore, but we also didn't want to know what was out there. Mei insisted no matter what she wasn't getting left alone. After some argument between all of us in four languages, Etta found a bag of bandages below her seat. We wrapped the rope burns on Mei's wrists and ankles in wet cloth. Cook fashioned together a giant sling from a bedsheet, and Omar hung the sling around his left shoulder.

We all went outside and while Omar stood rock-still, Mei climbed up him and sat herself in the sling with just a few quick steps, like a spider scaling leaves.

It was the kind of thing you wanna see twice to make it true. I think only me and maybe Cook, as the no-talent carnies, could really tell the magic in it. Etta nodded in tight approval. Simple Tom picked a snot from Simple Ben's nose, and ate it.

SEVEN.
It was one of the storage trucks that burned. All the trucks in our show were mostly kindling on top of a wheelbed, so it went up quick. The ashes sat now in a pile atop burst tires and blackened wheels. The surrounding grass was too green and wet to burn, so beyond the truck the flames hadn't spread. It wasn't clear what had started the fire. Lightning seemed the only possibility that made things less strange.

Other broken trucks and equipment littered the roadsides at intervals that seemed arranged. The acrobats and animals' trucks, but others too. There were torn up tents and rigging, and sideshow stand-ups smashed to pieces as if the magic in them had bled into the air.

Our group spread out to cover the grounds, like marking graves. No one spoke. As I walked, I thought I saw movement under each broken board. Little burned arms pulled themselves up from the grass with every breeze.

"Blow up," Omar said, and gestured with his hands. I nodded.

Mei hung off him with her knees locked in the sling. She reached to the ground to pick up the odd bit of flotsam and inspect it, before dropping it again as Omar strode through the debris.

"There's no midget truck, you know," Cook called out. We all looked at him. He stood in a pile of refuse.

"This is just ballerina shit," he said. "Tumbler shit."

He pointed to a tipped truck neaby. Across the side, painted acrobats flew through space over panels of burned wood. One twisted up young girl even looked a bit like Mei Shen. Cook stood out against this background like a wart.

"Midgets didn't travel with her," Cook said, and pointed at Mei Shen.

"She said she saw some burned-up midget. How'd she see some dead midget out here?" His hands went to his hips. "Some midget would have traveled with us in the freak truck anyways. I don't know no other place. She lost her mind."

"What he say?" Omar asked.

"He wrong. Here it was," Mei called out. "But not now."

We all walked over to where she was pointing, at a spot of ground no different from any other. But I saw the grass was matted here, and stained with black and rust.

We looked at Mei. She held up her fingers.

"It was here," she insisted.

I pictured small burned digits in my mind and looked at Etta, and she looked at me. I decided I should say something and opened my mouth to say it, wondering what it would be.

Ahead of us came a pair of shouts. Tom and Ben were flapping their arms as they ran at something giant and dark. It was so big I couldn't get a handle on it. We made our way forward, while in the distance the sky made threats.

Cook got to the twins first, and smacked Ben in the head so he cried. Then Cook looked down at whatever they'd been going on about.

"It's a big hole," he called out.

It was a big hole. What we'd seen from far off was a rim of upturned dirt that formed a soil wall. At its highest point the wall was maybe four feet, and then tapered off into a trench about fifty yards long and thirty feet across. It started away from the road to the west, then dug in around thirty feet deep before stopping in the center of the road. It was like the field was a wet sandbox and a giant child had scooped out a bucket's worth.

Tire treads ran away from the pit, toward where we stood and then past us. I looked behind me and saw that the tread ended where the burned-out hulk of the truck sat smoldering.

"Got hit," said Omar. "Lightning," he said, in case we were stupid.

So that was.

After running around in the hole for a minute getting covered in filth, Tom wanted out. But the sides of the pit were loose dirt with no handholds. He threw himself against the walls, screaming, while Ben stared down at him.

I sighed, then lay down on my stomach on the edge of the hole and reached a hand down. Tom ignored it. I sighed again.

Etta started talking soft to Tom, guiding him with her voice and her hand as she began to walk off the road, heading west into the field. Tom followed her, turning it into a game. He laughed and ran backward each time Etta moved toward him. As a group we walked this way from the road. A crop of knee-high wheatgrass blew here in patterns, ignorant of the leafless trees and dying fires in the road behind us.

Etta continued to call to Tom. She hadn't said thing one about finding her horses, I realized. They had to be the same pair Mei saw disappear into the storm.

Katya and Kolya, she called them. Purity and Victory. Etta was the only one of us who was brave, I thought then. Cook was a drunk, Omar was a fool, Mei Shen was half in shock.

And then Ben and Tom. And then me.

As Etta stood silhouetted against the clouds. I dug in my pocket for a cigarette. The wind blew Etta's hair around her face.

Up the hill Cook gave a shout and lifted something from the grass. We all winced, but it was just a painted flat with a lion's face on it, split halfway in two.

"Shit, where's the rest of it?" Cook called. "You think the

lions made it? You don't think there's lions out here, do you? Could animals have made it through that storm?"

"Horses survive," Mei Shen said.

"Not against lions," Omar said. He laughed. I grimaced and looked at Etta, but if Etta heard Omar she wouldn't say. She watched as Tom made his way out of the dirt pit and into Ben's arms, and they giggled at each other. I walked over to her, stepping fast with words coming up my throat, although I still wasn't sure quite what they'd be.

And then Omar was shouting, pointing uphill. We all followed his finger to a giant farmhouse at the top of the hill, with people milling around outside.

Omar and Cook yelled to one another, and Etta smiled too at seeing it. She looked to me as she led Ben and Tom toward us. I saw her trying to read my eyes. I wondered what it was she looked for there.

But I was looking past her back the way we came, seeing something in the trees that shouldn't have been there. It was another of our trucks, half-smashed with a giant painted lion's face, skidded into the brushline. The open end of it was aimed toward us.

In the dark of the truck was three sets of yellow eyes, looking back at me.

EIGHT.
The lions saw me seeing them between us and the way we came, and seemed in no rush to move. I turned to Etta and pointed out their truck, and first she squinted and then her eyes got wide. Cook looked too and said "shit," which was his answer to everything.

Omar was shouting about the house up the hill and why we needed to get to it, even though no one was against the idea.

"Omar!" I called out, and pointed down the hill. Tom and Ben were finally half-calm and didn't seem to understand most conversation, but I didn't wanna take a chance "lions" was part of their vocabulary.

Omar didn't get it, but Mei did and spoke low to him.

"Lions!" bellowed Omar. Etta grabbed Ben and Tom each by the hand and sung them some Russian nursery rhyme.

"So we go to house!" Omar said. "Not go back!"

"We're fine goin' to the house," I said. "Let's just move slow, all right? And hold off on the 'L' word."

"Fine, fine," he said, and headed up the hill.

Etta walked with Ben and Tom while me and Cook took rear, craning our necks back every other second. The lion truck was just a dark blot in the trees now. I had no way of knowing if those lions were there, or had disappeared in the tall brown grasses. Still, I was starting to feel silly about it when Cook stumbled over a rock and fell.

He cursed into the earth, but his rear stuck straight up and his drawers hung halfway off and when he went down he let loose a pretty considerable fart. I went to help him, but he rolled over like a pillbug and refused my hand until I swore I wasn't laughing at him.

"All right," I said, getting Cook stood. "Let's keep the pace."

"Fuck you!" Cook spat. "They ain't even movin'. Look, you can see 'em now."

Looking down the hill one more time I saw a big male lion perched atop the busted truck, stretched out with his paws dangling. I knew him. His name was Ferdinand. As I watched, he yawned.

Our lion tamer was out of northern California and called himself Claude VanDare. We put up with him because lions are a draw. He was third generation circus, and talked the history of the trade like it made him something to have the facts straight, even though the Europeans and Chinese went back seven generations, ten, a thousand years. One summer night when I was sitting outside my truck, Claude had come along carrying a cub. An hour later, he was still talking and I was learning more about lions than I thought I'd ever need.

"Misha and Rasha are our girls, but Ferdinand is the big boy," Claude said. He'd pointed vaguely off toward the lion cages at the other edge of the campground. "You know the boys ain't the ones you need to worry on, you know that. It's the females you gotta watch. First thing you learn. Males are big but they're dumb and mostly mane. The females—shit—they're ornery and too damn smart. We just keep 'em to make sure Ferdinand stays well-fucked."

Claude nursed the baby lion with a bottle of milk while he talked, and now he looked down to bounce the cub a little in his arm. Then he'd looked back and me and smiled through capped teeth.

"Were we all so lucky, right?" he said.

It was less than a year later Rasha took half Claude's arm.

Claude hadn't had a lot of fight in him after that. We'd left him in a hospital three states away. Now the lions were traveling with us to meet up with another trainer, but since the loss of Claude no one had much gone near them except to change their food and water.

I figured it made the lions about as sure of their place in that wheat field as we were. But in those long brown grasses, we were easy to spot. Couldn't say that much for the lions.

NINE.

My father worked as our town preacher, but he was not a pious man. He told the foulest jokes and the bluest stories, much the shame of my mother, who was more tightly wound. He loved being outside and especially he loved to hunt—not so much to trap or shoot, he said. Mostly just to be alone.

Once when I was a boy, my father took me out for the first day of deer season. We'd pulled off the road where the forest started just outside of town, and he'd led us to a hunting shack in a clearing about a mile from the highway. The shack was black with dew and cold, but I was excited to be alone with my father. While he set up his seat and a mini-cooler, I looked out at the damp forest around us.

When the morning warmed up I had to pee, and he pointed me toward a nearby grove of trees. The grove was in view of the shack, but I was shy. Once I got to the trees I decided to scoot around to the other side of the thicket for a little privacy.

The grove was bigger than it looked, and I had to walk a little bit before I found another trunk that looked good for emptying my bladder. Steam rose from the bark when I let loose, and a wave of relief ran over me. Then a shot rang out.

I froze and my stream went wild and splattered down my jeans. I just stood there with my peter in my hand, and a second shot slammed into a nearby trunk.

From a distance a voice was shouting, and as it came closer I heard my father, crashing through the brush, screaming "Fire! Fire!"

In one motion, he scooped me up, spun on his bootheel and whipped us back to the shack, my pants around my ankles, already crying, dribbling willy freezing in the open air.

We didn't do any more hunting that day, or for many more years. When my father got me home, he whipped me so good it hurt to sit down after.

I thought on this now as the sky cleared in that wheat field above the lion truck and the trees. A warm, hesitant sun snuck over us, the clouds patterned light across the meadows. The locusts rose again, clinging to the bent grasses and trilling low. Through their midst, the seven of us ran like hell.

It happened like this:

After curtailing a debate on lions and navigation, we'd headed again for the house at the top of the hill. I saw it held at least four stories, all misshapen. A tiny figure ran across the rooftop balcony. A shot rang out.

I was six years old in a hunter's field. I was twenty-some, sitting awake in some dark swamp.

We ducked and yelled. I stood up and almost yelled "Fire," when I saw the figure atop the house was waving at us.

Cook hit my back, saying "run, run, they's comin', run" and I realized "they" was lions and the shot was for them and that got me running too, jumping over furrows while behind us I heard galloping through the tall grasses.

But as we ran I was struck with the strangest feeling. My skin began to itch and tug at me, at my shoulders and along my spine.

It pulled me backward.

I was six years old and gutshot. I was twenty-some, skewered from behind a bayonet. I floated beneath the flattened gaze of an unblinking eye among black trees.

I thought of slowing my pace, of tripping, of dipping beneath the surf. I had been in bad times before and waited for my instincts to swing in, to remind my muscles I was a breathing fucking shitting machine of God. But my instincts were nowhere near. Instead I could only think to turn around and let the lions take me.

Etta ran ahead of me, her skin on fire, her head rimmed in light.

I followed after.

Pound pound pound pound and out, swatting insects from my face, hitting grass as another shot rang through, and I looked up and it was a wild old man standing on top of this ramshackle house, firing into nothing. I looked back into the wheatfield, and saw the tails of two lions running back the way we came.

Cook was clapping me on the back and laughing that we were alive and waving to the man on top of the house. An old woman called to us, saying they'd been watching the lions all morning.

Etta took my hand a moment, and that much felt good.

KEITH MCCLEARY

THE HOTEL.
TEN.
I have thought a few times since of one horrible jungle year. Our platoon was fragmented and moving south of the enemy camp, having missed our rendevous by an entire day. It was my first time in charge, but I'd lost my nerve. Without a plan, we'd walked in circles for hours or days through the undergrowth until an unexpected turn walked us into the middle of the camp we were supposed to be sneaking up on.

The other platoons coming in from north and east were already there. Every man was drunk and dancing with the local girls, whether or not the local girls were interested in dancing.

An officer ran up to us and gave me a big hug and shouted how glad he was we were alive. He said the mission was a botch all over and the entire regiment was waiting for orders. He asked if we'd run into problems in the jungle.

I suppose my boys were just as interested in not looking like fools as I was. We just nodded and said we'd gotten into some bad shit out there, yessir, bad shit. And the officer threw us a bottle of something, and that was that.

Another year, another war, another jungle, near the end of my last tour. My boys and I were buried in brush upriver from the firefight, checking on one of our own foxholes. It was low on food and hadn't seen reinforcement in weeks.

We came up on piles of dead men, three bodies deep all ways around, and the air smelled thick with smoke and gasoline. We called out a hello, then made our way into the trench.

It was like crawling into a crypt full of living folk. The foxhole dripped with fetid water and loose-packed muck, sounds getting muted as we dropped below the earth. Wood held the walls back from caving, but they were rotten and a stink rose from the planks. We found our men, but something in them was deeply wrong. Their eyes were sunken half-moons, their hair and beards matted like rats drowned in shit. They barely spoke, but low moans escaped their throats.

I was already dying inside by then—my wife had left me, taking a daughter I feared I might never meet—and I felt like I'd cursed those boys somehow, just by them being in my charge.

I snapped present. Someone was touching me, leading me, but I was just arms and legs moving. A windowed back door opened, and we were ushered from gray skies and wheat fields into a cave of familiar faces turned wary and dark.

Whatever it had been before, the back of the strange house on the hill was now a way station for carnies. The wood-paneled mudroom was full of the weak and infirm. Teamsters, jugglers, acrobats, and the bearded lady all stared at me. My mind flickered on drunken AWOL soldiers, and the sad stares of long dead boys down the foxhole, surrounded by dirt and stink.

Warm hands reached for Simple Tom and Ben. Etta and Cook got circled too. Voices rose in a wave. The shadows of carnies formed the faces of people I knew, with names I couldn't place. Comfort and discussion rushed forth in several languages while I stood aside.

I caught snatches of conversation. Wrecked trucks separated by the storm had not been our unique experience, nor had whatever strange abuse Mei Shen had suffered. But concern about what was to be done next was beginning to take hold. The warm feelings all around were tinged with worry, and frightened grins got too close.

I was shook with a hand like an old claw, and turned to see a hunched wrinkled woman standing next to me.

"Let me wash you up, old son," she said. Leathered fingers whispered on my skin, pulling me from the mass.

I stepped back from the circus folk and turned and followed a withered gray head from the back room through a swinging door. I'd only just adjusted to the dimlit house, when light hit my eyes again.

I stood in a sunny country kitchen. It was yellow and white here and a low breeze blew in from a small window. The old woman caught the door behind me and closed it firm against the brook of conversation on the other side. She beckoned to me.

I was made to sit on a stool and the old woman stood next to me, no more than four feet tall. She wore an apron, and her white hair was combed back over her head. Her eyes were deep-set and half-closed. She looked at me, then turned to rinse a washcloth.

"That's a nasty bump," she said. She wrung out the cloth and pressed it to my temple and my whole face woke at once. I sucked in air as the rag came away with spots of blood.

"I didn't know I got bumped," I said.

"Ayuh," she said, not unkind. "We can get you washed off anyway."

She took a look down my arm and across my chest at the ink dug in there.

"You're circus folk too, then?" she asked.

"That or these are some bad birthmarks," I said.

She sniffed, and her smile fell. In the hallway past her, someone laughed, but the laugh was shrill.

"Well, I'm out of beds," she said. "'Less folk start shackin' up triple, which they may have to. I ain't figgered if the men should stay with the women, tho."

We were in an alcove, while straight ahead it opened to real line kitchen with two stoves, a walk-in pantry, and an icebox.

With enough food, you could cook for an army here, a hundred out-of-towners, or a gaggle of downtrodden carnies.

"This a hotel?" I said.

"Boardinghouse. Me n' husband run it," the woman said, dotting my forehead. "You're all lucky. We lost our renters when locust season started. The storms have kept new folk from comin' through. Then you start showin' up."

"How long they been coming?" I said.

She pursed her lips. "Since after breakfast, I suppose. Clouds cleared after the rain last night, and we look out the window to see folks in costume coming up the fields. Ain't never seen such a thing. You all looked so lost, like babies. We just started scooping you up. S'pose I would have thought twice, if I'd known how many of you there'd be."

Her hands moved roughly across my face, cleaning off blood and dirt. "I didn't plan on triple a room and no one's ante'd up to pay for anything," she said. "So you're double lucky I have a sweet heart."

"I don't doubt it," I said. "Our ringmaster'll show up looking for his show. Name's Frank. He'll have money."

"The promise of a painted man, that I'll take," she said. "You'll need to clean your shirt. I'll see what we can find you, once things are settled."

I said my thanks, and the old woman walked back out to look for other circus folk in need of attention. I wondered at each band of carnies finding themselves that morning spread across the county in states of distress. I wondered too if boardinghouses across the countryside had scooped them up, or if there was only one road we all were lost on, and it led only here.

The kitchen had another door at the opposite end, and that end seemed quieter. I decided to head that way.

In a moment I found myself in the front of the house. There wasn't much to the interior. The ground floor, except for the carnies, was empty. There was at least some furniture, but otherwise it was just a big dark room with fat wooden pillars leading to the ceiling. A fireplace sat against one wall, with chairs and a table set up around it. It was like a farmhouse that wanted to be a hotel but didn't quite know how.

The far side of the room was a staircase leading to upper floors, and the front wall was windows that looked onto a grassy lawn, with dirt road and fields beyond. The staircase groaned, and an old man came down, white-haired and stooped in pale overalls, carrying a mop and bucket. He stopped at the landing and looked up at me, then passed me toward the kitchen.

Husband, I guessed.

I crossed the length of the front room and stepped outside onto a small porch. The sun had fallen behind a cloud and the air was cool, the light soft and gray.

To my right, the road rolled down a hill, then back up again into forest and cow fields and countryside. To my left, the road fell steep into a hamlet—a cluster of houses, a few stores and a church. If this was Pickinpaw, it seemed smaller than the circus itself.

My skin pricked all over, and made it hard to think. Perhaps Frank would be here soon, and maybe then my head would clear enough to put names with faces for the other carnies. I needed a cigarette but didn't want to talk to anyone enough to ask. I thought if I stood in one spot long enough, the universe might get willed into giving me a smoke.

ELEVEN.

I woke up and it was dark and I smelled beans.

Etta was sitting over me. She wore a summer dress. I realized she'd been stuck in her carnival outfit since the morning. Now she had a plate in her hand that smelled spicy and rich, but still was beans.

I tried to move and pain arched my back like a newborn crying. I'd fallen asleep in the middle of the boardinghouse's front yard, with my head on a tree root. Everything ached.

"Shit," I said.

"Up," Etta said. She gave me a plate. It had beans and a potato on it.

I sat up. I ate.

Light shown from the other side of the house. Past Etta was a tent on the sidelawn, with a long table and pots of food. Carnies were eating, talking, wandering in and out the dark. Even sat across the grass I felt the anxiousness on them. It chewed at the corners every time we went off schedule or had a break between shows, much less a complete breakdown in the middle of nowhere.

My fork scraped nothing and I saw the food was gone. Something shifted in my back pocket. I found a pair of cigarettes I'd rolled, gave one to Etta, then lit us both.

There was a small thicket of bushes behind us that grew up from beneath the porch. We moved to sit behind them.

"Thanks for the food," I said.

Etta blew smoke. "You need to stop sitting on your cigarettes."

"You could have woke me up off the lawn," I said.

"Hell no," Etta said. "You fight when you sleep."

We spent a moment watching the rabble.

"So what's the word?" I asked.

"We were last to come," Etta said. The Russian made boxes and fences around her words. "But only half circus showed up. Missing teamsters, mimes. Animals."

"Except the lions and horses," I said. "And no one misses a mime."

I counted heads. "Still seems like a lot of people, for us missing folk," I said.

"We supposed to be picking up more people at the next town," said Etta. "Their trucks get smashed in storm, they made it here too. So now we have less of us, more of them."

"Who's feeding everyone?" I asked.

"Cook, and the old lady who is here," said Etta. "Already they hate each other."

"Course they do," I said. I took a drag. "Frank get here?"

Etta nodded, took a puff, and didn't look at me. The night cooled.

I couldn't let a thing alone.

"How's he?" I asked. Etta shrugged.

"He is stressed," she said. "This is bad, you know? We have no show." I saw her hand was shaking too. "I think he doesn't know what to do."

"Do you?" I said.

She looked at me funny. "What do you mean?"

"Nothing," I said. She looked at me again, then looked away.

Men's voices shouted from inside the house behind us. Etta stiffened, tossed her butt, and smiled thin at me. Then she stood, and brushed herself off, and walked away.

I watched her walk across the yard until she disappeared. Then I got up, stretched, flicked my ash. I picked at the tobacco off my tongue.

Something started laughing like a pig and a wolf both, and I peered into the back lawn to see Cook sitting there, leaned against the house. A flask hung in his hand and he grinned at me.

"Poor old Sue," he said. "You gon' be blueballed fo' life, boy, long as you hang 'roun that woman. Ain't no future outside yo' bunk!"

"All right," I said. Cook bore on.

"She the ringmaster's girl!" he squealed. "She got no use for you, and Frank would kill you anyhow! What you gotta offer, boy? Whatchoo got? Ha haaaaa!"

"Christ, shut up, you old fuck," I said, and walked off before I could kill him in the dark. The makeshift slop tent on the side of the house was overfull of people and light. I turned to the front steps of the house, and headed in.

TWELVE.

The voices I'd heard from outside got louder as I walked inside, and the screen door swung behind me. A long table had been set up in the empty room, with chairs gathered round it under a single hanging lamp. Our hosts had gone to bed, but carnies keep odd hours. There were four men at the table and one pacing around it, all lit from above in yellow hues.

"I don't see it," said Papa Canelli. Canelli was old circus. His sons were jugglers, the daughters acrobats, and his youngest boy performed with Papa and his wife in a dog act with maybe a thousand-and-a-half beagles, where the dogs ran around Canelli while he bounced his guts in a fancy jacket.

That jacket hung unbuttoned now around his shoulders. Bean juice stained his undershirt.

"I don't see it," Papa said again. "What you saying? That we carry on'a show with no crew an' half the acts? What we gonna show, eh? Ripped costumes an' muddy tents? We have to fin' who's missing! Someone must know somethin'! The ground didn't swallow dem up!"

"Of course not," said another man with a light tan suit and a white handlebar moustache. "But we have to trust the local police. I know a lot of people in this town. Good men. You let them do their jobs."

I remembered from the afternoon a man on the roof had scared the lions off with rifleshot, and decided now that this was him. He seemed civilian despite his carny look.

"Mr. Nelson is right, Antonio," said a third voice. "Hell, we can't find those men on a good night in Tahoe when we need 'em for breakdown. How're we going to find 'em now? What we can do is put on a show, get some money an' haul out."

The third man was our ringmaster, Frank Colt.

Frank Colt was a young man, a good-looking man—too young and too good-looking to run a show, folks said. So that was. Frank was tall and lean and arrogant, but no more than you'd expect. He was boss and ringmaster, but not aware of much.

On the nights Etta weren't with me, she was with Frank.

This wasn't a deal Frank was clear on, far as I knew.

So that was.

Fourth at the table was some kind of human snake, leaned way back in his chair, sitting in shadow.

"Putting on a show, Mr. Colt," said the snake, "Is the right idea."

Maybe not a snake. Just a trick of the light. He was tall and thin and all right angles, with a purple topcoat over a purple suit, and a tophat sat next to him on the table. He out-circused the rest of us, and seemed bored doing so.

He turned toward me now, eyes flat in the light, and smiled with lips pulled back on his teeth. I remembered the stranger on the road that morning. The day, twisted since it started, settled now all sewed together wrong.

"Hello, Sue," the interloper said.

Frank Colt turned around to look at me, and a waft of cigar smoke was released, like the energy of the men at the table had contained the air and now broke apart. Frank's eyes flicked over me in a way that would have made me twitch, had I not been eyeballed many times before. The others looked too, and I held ground as they sniffed me out.

"Hey there, Sue," Frank finally said. He turned back to the violet suit behind him. "How you know Sue there, Alphonse? You all met before?"

The man's eyes stayed locked. "We've exchanged hellos. I believe I heard his name tossed around today by that horse-rider he came in with." He smiled. "Ain't that right? Ain't that who you come in with?"

"That's right," I said. His stare sank through me.

"Oh, right," said Frank. "Etta." He laughed. "Hell, Sue! Way I figure you saved her life! Or she saved yours! What you figure, she save you or you save her?" He smiled. "I owe you one for bringin' back my girl, Sue. Come and have you a drink."

I sat down in a wicker chair about six inches too low. Frank poured me a glass of whiskey and passed it over.

"We was just discussin' with Mr. Ambrose here the fact that we're in shit city," Frank said. Next to him was Tillinger, a teamster who doubled as Frank's snitch. Right now Tillinger was red-nosed and blind and bobbling in his seat.

"Shit city!" Frank said again, and Tillinger belched beer.

"You work for the show, yes?" asked the white-moustached fella that had been pacing back and forth. "Teamster, are you?"

"Sue's on the freak truck," said Frank. The elder man peered across the table at my arms.

"Oh, I see," he said. "Yes, of course."

"Don't know how you put up with it, Sue," Frank said. "You're the only one a'thems not a mutant or a retard. Sue gets the rest a'them oddjobs in line. King of the freaks, he is." Then, to Tillinger: "King of the freaks!"

I looked at the moustached gentleman across the table. "Believe I owe you thanks. You were shootin' from the top of the house when we were comin' in."

"Oh yes," the fellow said. "The lions. We'll get those buggers soon enough; not much for them to hunt around here except rabbits. I hope we find them before they attack the locals."

He walked around the table to me. "You're Sue? Another

man cursed with a woman's name. Lindsay Nelson," he said, sticking out his hand. "I run the other circus teaming up with Frank's. Stewarded it, really, till Frank could take it over. Never was a thing I ran too well." And he laughed.

I shook his hand, and then reached for another drink. Mr. Nelson continued to stand too close to me. "I'm a collector of odd names," he said. "I can't say I've heard Sue on a man before, though. Very interesting."

I poured from the bottle, threw back a second glass, and looked at him through red eyes.

"Right," I said. "Well."

Lindsay resumed his tour of the table. The purple-suited snake was looking at me now. Grinning.

"And you know Mr. Ambrose," Frank was saying.

A hand slid in front of me.

"Alphonse Ambrose," said the violet-suited man.

I shook the hand once, and it was smooth just like any hand would be. But the eyes of him.

"Mr. Ambrose is one a'my investors," said Frank Colt. "Comin' up to help us square the deal with Mr. Nelson here, and catching us with our pants down!" Frank laughed again, thin.

"Acts of god are no one's fault," said Ambrose. "And why they come, no one can know."

And he sat back in his chair and looked at Frank, and at Tillinger, and Lindsay Nelson.

Then at me.

"The storm busted up most of the riggings—that is, what little was found," he said. "The performers are mostly passed out in the rooms upstairs, or in shock—those few who've shown up at all. It seems we're all out of ideas on what to do next, Sue." As he spoke, his lips made shadows.

"What you got?" he said. His eyes made shadows too.

When I'm working, eyes on me are easy. I set up in a wooden chair and the world slows and the eyes, voices, customers are like waves and I let time go. Sometimes I'll walk the tent freely, and on occasion a child comes up terrified, but wanting to see the tattoos.

Where did you get them all? The child will ask, and I kneel down so they can touch my arms, see it's skin just like what they got. If I have a parrot on my shoulder, they may want to see it too, but I tell them to hang back and keep their hands safe. Me they can touch, and I got critters plenty—crawling across my shoulders, back and chest.

I been all over the world, I say. All over the world and I got a picture on me everywhere to remind myself where I been.

These are words I've memorized. Someday I'll say them to you.

You're so good with animals, the mothers always say. Do they bite? Not that it matters to you; I suppose the ink stung worse, huh?

That ink don't feel nothin', I say, and we breathe each other in. That's when the ink pulls at me. It knows these small-town women, and that there'd be no consequence.

But in my life, there ain't never been a lack of consequence.

I thought now on roaming eyes and roaming hands. The question I'd been asked hung like the smoke in the room. Ambrose stared steady at me.

"That storm fucked us good," I said. "What did y'all come up with so far?"

"As I've said," Lindsay Nelson began like no one else was in the room, "Letting the local authorities find your missing performers is the quickest thing. In the meantime, we'll do what we can with what we have."

"'We, we'!" said Papa Canelli. "All this time this man says we! It is us," Canelli said, his finger pointing around the table, "And you!" and here he pointed at Lindsay.

"Nevertheless," Mr. Nelson replied, "Until tonight I owned half this circus. I believe my opinion on how best to capitalize on your misfortune should be taken well in hand."

"Lindsay's right, Signore," said Ambrose to Canelli. "He has a point about making a little money here. Treat it like real ol' time carny—a few acts, a few tricks. What do you say, Frank?"

Frank looked at Ambrose, then at me.

"Sue? You're a thoughtful man. What do you think?" Frank said. His eyes were half in his drink. I couldn't tell if I was being set up or condescended to, or something else. Frank didn't seem himself. He just seemed rattled.

"Well," I said, "We'll have to paint the town red gettin' a good turn out for whatever show we put on. But we ain't got enough trucks right now to go nowhere else. I guess you could do a little dog n' pony while we see if we can find the other carnies. We shown up. Figure they will too."

I sat back. Unless they're dead. Unless the storm swallowed them.

Frank looked at the group like he'd said my words. "Hell, that's three votes. The logic's sound. My vote's four."

Silence hung around the table.

"Settled then. Thanks, Sue." Frank said, and laughed, and they all laughed. I smiled with them. Frank held up an empty bottle and looked back to Linsday Neslon. "Mr. Nelson, do you have another bottle of this excellent whiskey?"

Lindsay Nelson twitched, and nodded. "I believe I can find another."

"Y'all don't mind," I said, and stood. "It's been a long day."

"Ain't gonna have another drink with us, Sue? Well all right," Frank said. Nelson reappeared with a second bottle, and there were cheers as Frank began to pour.

With nothing else to do, I decided to take the stairs up to the second floor. Each step groaned, but not loud enough to mask a voice that slid across the house toward me.

"Good meeting you, Sue," said Alphonse Ambrose in my ear. "Much obliged."

THIRTEEN.

The house was big, and when you hit one part of it the rest disappeared. As I touched the landing to the second floor, talk from the men downstairs fell to a rumble and then was gone. To my left, a slim window cast a glow on the floorboards. I looked down through the glass and saw clusters of folk—teamsters getting drunk, younger girls doing a balance show for the horse groomers standing nearby. Pairs of carnies stretched out on the lawn like a late-night holiday. I sat down on the stairs and took another look.

As I slumped against my forearms I saw folks below I didn't recognize. You run into every tumbler, juggler, peepshow and one-man band at least a few times in this business, and even when you move up a rung you find them bottom-feeders got hired up right with you. As I looked now, new faces mingled with the old. I wondered where Nelson had brought his circus from.

I saw Marvelous Ling, a dish-spinner out of Frisco who was only decent to be around when he was loaded. I saw a puppetman who'd got sweet with me in a bar in Saginaw to no good end, and a young gaggle of identical triplets I'd worked with a hundred times without knowing what they did.

I saw Omar too, sniffing around them girls with a smile

on his face that turned my guts. I pounded the window, once. Omar didn't look up. I pounded twice, again.

He stopped and craned his neck around and that gave the trio time to wander outside his range. I watched as Omar got himself turned and talking to another woman. Her body language said she could handle herself better than the triplets would have, and she threw her head back and walked away from him.

As her face hit the lamplight the sight of her cooled my skin. The posters called her Serena the Snake Woman. No wonder Omar'd been refused. I worked on breathing. Knowing Serry, Omar got off easy.

Minutes crawled by. I heard chairs pull out and grunts below, steps across the floor and on the landing. As I sat by the window, Frank came up around the steps toward me, sliding against the wall.

He stopped, feeling someone else was there.

"Shit, Sue," he said. He lurched on me, grabbed my undershirt, and dangled there. I'd seen Frank drunk before, and knew mostly he'd just babble. I set in to wait him out.

But he just stared me. His face rippled and he smiled.

"Tell me you'll save me from these people, Sue," Frank said.

The smile flickered away again.

I eyed him over. He smelled of drink and filth and flop sweat.

"Sure, Frank," I said. "It'll be all right, anyway."

He nodded slow, once and again.

"Fuck it will," he said. He smiled a second time, then patted my chest. Between each pat, his hand strayed on me longer, till he was holding me by my shirt again. The resting fingers curled, and twisted, and he was squeezing a ball of fabric in his fist. He looked over my shoulder.

We sat awhile like that in the dark. His black eyes went straight inside him. He licked his lips and his tongue clicked inside his mouth.

"We all go down together," he said.

His whole face shook. He slumped, let go. Then he stood. "I know you," he said. "Think I don't. There's no bed up there. Other side the house."

And he smiled a third time, and stumbled past me.

I breathed out.

So that was.

It hit me sudden. Ling, the puppet-man, Serry and Omar, Frank fallen down a well. The odd man Nelson, and storms, and mixing carnies. And Mei Shen, and Cook, and Etta. And Ambrose, snake-tongued in the room below, in this house up a hill to nowhere, his arrival like a storm itself. I felt something bad growing worse between us, taking time to piece together.

I told myself I was just drunk and sad, and things would look better in the morning. I wanted Etta to find me, but knew she wouldn't. Hell, I was lucky she'd been brave enough to serve me beans.

I sat a long time on the landing, looking out the window and feeling like nothing, the whiskey humming behind my eyes.

FOURTEEN.

The slick darkness of the upstairs hung over the corridors. Creaks and groans echoed from other rooms. I imagined clowns and tumblers piled on one another like stacks of old clothes.

At the end of one dark hallway, I found a small room with a small window, a sagging mattress, and a closet door. It seemed as though someone had forgotten this entire part of the house. I lay down and my mind spiraled out, unlocking black tendrils of worry that rolled across the floorboards and stuck to the walls.

I thought of Etta. I saw her sitting in front of her makeup mirror, fitting her domino mask, touching her hair helmeted into place with pins and spray. I saw the healthy flesh of her back sliding into her costume, smelled the night smells of crowd and air. I imagined her now in one of the far rooms, awake next to the stinking drunk of Frank. I wondered if she thought of me as I did her.

I thought of Serry too. Her eyes chewed at the bad thoughts I carried with me, waking them and rattling their chains.

I'd been pointed to Coney Island after I was discharged, and started on labor jobs until someone said I might make a buck as an illustrated man. I followed directions from the carnies to a three-story brick castle off the boardwalk. Inside was a dancehall on the first floor, a noisy theater on the third. I thought

Noah's Ark had gotten beached and loaded with freaks, then left to bake in this place where I'd run aground myself.

The lady of the house was a half-dwarf named Nan who chain-smoked and wore a wool suit. She said, "You need more ink, but you you can work. You put half each paycheck to more tattoos, I'll get you started with a paintjob in a dark room."

I said sure.

I got the ink done for weeks after. My new self had no history, just regret. I sat afternoons and nights on the boardwalks, doing what was needed, healing from my wounds and talking to anyone who didn't try too hard to know me. The eye I'd seen out in the jungle still hung overhead, watching as I tried to throw a life together.

I'd been like that four months when I met Serena the Snake Woman.

She'd come up on me one night between the shows. I'd moved from our tent down to the beach where the surge came in and carved out the shape of the island, and made me think of wars and borrowed time.

I smoked and the tobacco fuzzed out the light and sound from the carnival shows. I looked down the coast and saw a woman slinking along the tide. From my spot I watched her move like a balance of spheres. After crossing in front of me about thirty yards off, she found a stairway leading back to the boardwalk. The glow hit her and I saw she only wore a fitted two-piece, with makeup and glitter-paint on her shoulders and thighs. It was slick enough that I figured her for carny, and not one of the islanders, who were no small shakes themselves in measure of weirdness.

The cig ran to my fingers and I watched the ash, wondering when it might start to burn and if I might want one more. Then a shadow was hanging over me.

"Your name really Sue?" Her body was muscle and a long neck and a face all hard angles, with black eyes framed in makeup glazed green. Her skin was painted like mine, but hers would clean off in the morning.

"Here it is, yeah," I said. I tried not to drink her in.

"So somewhere else it's not?" she asked, and sat down next to me. She smiled out the side of her mouth, and heat rose off her.

"Somewhere else it's not," I said.

She snorted. I could have pulled her hair back and poured myself into her face.

"Whatever you say," she said.

"You come out here for me?" I asked. She nodded her head the way she came.

"Nan's lookin' for you," she said. "Their geek's home drunk and she needs a fill-in."

I shook my head. "I told her I don't geek," I said. "That's bad business."

"You never geeked? You're too good for it? Gimme," she said, and I cigged her.

"Good nothing," I said. "I ain't got it in me for killin' chickens. I'm a plain coward."

She pursed her lips and looked me over. By then my skin was well filled. Only needed the last few pieces to make it whole, and they'd come later, when I'd find out what being done with killing was really all about.

"I don't see you as the yellow type," she said. "Too good for it, that's you."

"However you cut it," I said. "I ain't no geek."

She took a drag. "I done it," she said, and smiled again as my eyebrows raised. "Bit the heads off snakes," she said, and mimed the act. "Then spit 'em with a blood capsule, rubbed 'em on my tits." She leaned back. "It's good money, but it's a mess."

I looked at her again and knowing dawned. "Now I got you. Ain't you a snake charmer at this show?"

She nodded. "Sometimes I forget where I'm at and try to bite one still." She laughed and stood. "Nan said you'd be pussy, but she wants you to find her anyways."

Nan was a tough bird, but she didn't deserve what happened to her in the end.

"I'll come by," I said. "Who do I say sent me?"

For a moment, the woman looked charmed. Then it passed.

"Serry," she said. "We'll see each other around." And she turned with a twist of her thigh, boots clicking as she left.

She was right on that. Even if she wasn't, I would have found some kind of trouble either way. Maybe not so bad or bloody, but things always went wrong, real wrong, back then. Some people just can't wait to be human wreckage.

FIFTEEN.
 I woke hours later in the boardinghouse back room. The ink had got to me, scratching and digging underneath my skin, gnawing my neck and forcing my eyelids off my eyes. I came to with my jaw clenched, veins hot.
 A silhouette sat on the edge of the bed, rimmed in moonlight. I pulled back, tucking my feet.
 "I didn't know I'd find you here," she said.
 I heard Etta's accent in her words, and Serry's alto growl. Between them was something else I couldn't place.
 "But here I am," I said. The room was warm, the sheets slick with sweat.
 "There's something you should see," she said. She wore a white gauze gown and through it I could see the curves of her, the shadows breathing over breastbone.
 "What you mean?" I said. I wondered who she was, why I couldn't see her face. She spoke with so many different voices, and I felt space between them.
 "Look," she said.
 I looked out the little window to the lawn below. It was lit by a cool full moon. In the grasses I saw a figure walking, and as I squinted I made out the old man I'd met that afternoon with mop and bucket. He stumbled as I watched, then fell into the grass.

"Shit," I said.

And we were running to the lawn, clamoring down back stairs and through the house that at night seemed only dust and cobwebs. I think I knew that I was dreaming but there were important things here, things I couldn't see quite clear.

We hit the lawn, she and I, ran to the old man and dragged him by his ankles back inside, and as we did I heard lions in the fields beyond, their hunger crawling toward me and we couldn't save our cargo fast enough. The old man would not wake up.

The animal sounds grew closer. In the night the locusts rose, swarms blotting out the moon. Around us the forest screamed and the shadows came.

We could no longer lift his limbs. As blackness crawled across his body, we turned and ran for the boardinghouse. We left him there beneath the moon.

And me and this woman and the darkness watching, so soaked in sweat we couldn't think—we took each other there. She undressed me of the pictures in my flesh, freeing me of the weight I'd borne.

I think we were there on that bed, in that old tiny room on a soiled stained sinking mattress, parts of her in my mouth and parts of me in hers and then sleeping, sleeping, wrapped round each other and pulled away, sleeping sleeping like sinking ships. When I woke it would be to skin scratched clean, a million little cuts, and someone was in bed with me, and someone was shouting, and I could not decide if I felt more absolved or guilty for the things I didn't know yet that I had done.

THE LIONS.
SIXTEEN.
The morning light hung flat in the little room. Thumps on the stairs ruptured.
I slid a hand over my face as my troubles found me. Something rattled, something rotten. Food smells hung in the air, burned and soured. The room was getting hot.
I stood, stretched, and turned to see Serry lying in bed, looking odd at me.
"Shit," I said.
She smiled.
"Sorry," I said.
"Shhhh," she said. She sat up, skin tanned and oily, the big mess of brown hair like a city on her head. She stood and threw a robe over. I felt like an invader to this place.
"You stare and stare, I remember that," she said with a half-smile. I began to speak, but she looked at me like a glimpse in a broken rearview.
"Don't worry, Sue. It's just one room," she said, and slipped out the door.
I stood awhile, naked and hot, feeling the dust settle into the cuts and scratches she'd left in my skin. The ink buzzed across my shoulders, denying forgiveness.
I became aware of the world outside the room, sounds

outside and below. My gut followed the smell of food and got me dressed, and got me out.

I walked downstairs and stood again on the landing, now in sunlight. Even that felt strange. I could imagine this was my landing in my house, with a yard and wife and child. I could place myself into these things, as if they weren't lost and littered across counties and states so I might never gather them again.

The strange dreams of the night before hung on me, struggling to connect. I saw Frank's face, lost in moonlight.

Damn Serry. Damn my bed.

SEVENTEEN.

The downstairs of the house looked much as it had the day before—large and empty. But I had the feeling there was a morning I had missed. Voices echoed from the backyard.

I looked in on the kitchen as I passed it. It was empty too, but pans were sprayed across the countertop in a pattern I recognized. Cook had been here, but whatever he'd done was burned now and abandoned.

There was a wailing that came in through the windows, and as I stepped over the threshold onto the back lawn I was swarmed with color and sound. The sun lit up the grass electric green and the sky sang blue and the fields orange. I wondered how I'd slept as long as I did.

Cook was sitting and drinking by the door, and carnies gathered round trying to block things off. But the wailing continued and I saw it was the the old lady of the house, fallen to her knees, retching solid grief.

Out there in the field under a cloth stained with blood, something was ripped up and misshapen. I'd seen enough dropcloths to know when some dead fool was under one. I could see the tiny arthritic hand, all tense and scrabbling at the crabgrass, poking out from underneath the cloth. The cloth itself was a maze of gore beneath the fabric, like the meat and gristle it covered was punished into the ground for being alive. The old lady of the house knelt by what was left, knees wet with dew, her wail falling into silence, sucking in air and coughing out the dust inside her. Several of our bigger men circled her like you would a rabid cat.

"What happened here," I said, not asking but saying.

"Lions," said Cook. "Lions got the husband in the night."

My dreams the night before swam into focus. My skin sang to me. I heard an old gypsy saying most of what she did was hoodoo. I saw the long unblinking eye.

My feet carried me forward while my body hung back. Farther past the bloodied grass were Lindsay Nelson and Frank Colt, waving off bugs and watching over the grasslands that led to the wreckage of trucks and tents in the trees.

"I think with the ruckus last night he passed out on the lawn and got left out here," Lindsay was saying. "Then—well."

"Meat wagon and police is a town over," Frank said. "Til they come, here we are."

"We'll simply have to comb the fields," Lindsay said. "We make a grid and cover all of it. Between yours and my rifles, we'll be armed enough."

I thought on truths lying down with untruths. I stood there dumb as my heart began to beat again.

"Hell," I said. The two men turned to me and looked me over.

"Morning," Nelson said to me. "Terrible thing. Can you fire a gun, Sue?"

I looked at him, turning slow.

"Sure," I said.

"Weren't you overseas, Sue?" said Frank. "Didn't Etta say somethin' about that?"

"Sue, you're ex-brass?" Lindsay said. "You don't say." He rolled across me with his eyes. "Hell, I'm getting distracted," he said. "Listen, this is bad business. We've got deputies from two towns around het up over this. When they get here, we'll need to comb the lions out of those fields."

Then he nodded to us, and walked back toward the house. Frank moved to follow him.

I grabbed Frank's arm. "You're taking down the lions? They're just animals. They don't know what they done."

"Tranque-darts, Sue," said Frank. He was sober, but now we were alone and his eyes were just as hollow as they'd been the night before. "Those lions are the most valuable thing this show's got going. We get them first, make the locals happy, then piece together the rest before the dog n' pony on the weekend."

I processed all that and grabbed Frank's arm. "Hell man, we just need to leave here," I said. "Once them lions is caught. We've poisoned the well. You ain't gonna have a show."

Frank spun on me, eyes still sober but now a flat black too.

"I still have a circus spread across this county, Sue. Two of them, as it stands. I never let a bad day stop me, and I'm not starting now. Get upstairs and eat." He took his arm back and pointed above us, then went inside.

I looked up to my right and saw a large wooden porch built off the house's second floor. Above me were the rest of the carny folk, eating breakfast with indifference. I found myself wondering briefly if the house's architecture shifted as needed, reforming itself where it perched.

EIGHTEEN.

We watched the meatmen come and scrape up the ravaged pieces that had been the old woman's husband. Police came too, but they knew even less what to do about lions than we did. The carnies hung back, eating the breakfast put out for them by Cook on the wooden patio up the hill. One of the teamsters, big and gruff and drunk by noon, hooked up a hose to wash the grass of blood.

Last night's dream still made trails across my brain. I lit a cigarette and hid in smoke as the Simple Twins were fed their jelly and peanut butter, as Omar and Serry came out together with some of the other sideshows, throwing back their liquor early. Our small army was taking over the house like an invading plague, and that everyone seemed so comfortable with this arrangement seemed the strangest part.

Lindsay Nelson and Frank stood below us, nodding to two deputies as they assessed the fields. While the carnies hunkered next to me in rumbling quiet, I saw Etta as she entered and sat with the other horse-folk.

"Watch those eyes, Sue," a voice said. Serry had paused nearby, and was following my gaze. Her tone was almost kind.

I grunted back and Serry shook her head, then wandered

off. From across the room Etta looked at me. Her face was sad and blank.

The food in my stomach was dust. Down through the trees I could see the thumbprint of black dirt where we'd found the long, deep ditch the morning prior. It sat still like a testament, or a warning. Like a shadow that would not move.

NINETEEN.

We all got real busy staying clear of things when the police took aside Frank Colt and Lindsay Nelson to help plan how to catch the lions. With Frank and Lindsay gone, the tink-tink, tink-tink of silverware on plates and a slow mumble of chatting carnies fell soft on the patio and in the small country dining room just inside.

I was sitting in the dining room when Cook wandered up and nodded, then slumped beside me. From across the room, Papa Canelli smiled a conspiracy, then crossed and sat down too.

"There's you," he said. "Where you sleep, Sue? How you avoid craziness this morning, eh?"

"I sleep heavy," I said, and he laughed too big.

"Not what I hear, eh?" and he winked. I leveled an eye at him. "Oh, I kid you," he said. "What you think all this? Big mess, eh?"

"Big mess," I said.

Canelli leaned in, still smiling.

"I think we got to get hell out of dodge, eh?" he said. "Stick aroun' here, bad business. Got a bad stink all over it. You know one girl, Chinese—she was all tied up! Wake up in a ditch!"

"That was Mei Shen," I said. "She was some mess all right. She okay?"

"Ach sure, now," Canelli said. "Bruises, arms, legs. My wife saw her, clean her up. She can't remember anything! Why this happening? Not just storm out there, no!"

Papa pulled out a smoke, lit it, and turned his chair to look into the fields.

"Not just storm out there," he said again. "Something else."

He pointed to the end of the hedgerow, just beyond the treeline. A couple things stood out from this distance. The bright reds and yellows of the smashed trucks was one. The other was the large black furrow in the earth.

"I talk to that old woman yesterday," Papa was saying. "That hole out there. She say that not there before the storm. Show up when we did." He turned to me, still with the smile. "We have been marked, you know? By God." He laughed all queer, then gave a wave and looked back down into the fields.

He looked at me again, losing the smile. "What's out there?" he said. "Highwaymen? Animals? Devils? Don't matter. We leave, that's what matters. Best we roll on out soon as we can, I think."

"You better talk to Frank on that," I said.

"Ain't no way we're gonna have a show here," Cook said. He leaned forward, and his eyes crawled up his face to look across the table.

"No, Sue is right," said Papa. "His voice dropped low. "He will say we stay. Put on show, make bucks, then we leave."

Papa Canelli nodded, eyes closed. As he did, a few of his broodlings came through, chasing each other like meadowlarks, and jumped on him. He spun around to shout Italian at his wife, who'd just stepped outside, and she shouted back at him.

With the Canellis came a few others that had been holed up in the house somewhere, flushed out like sewage. The movement caused ripples around us. Omar emerged, and snaked near our table.

Papa kept talking. "We have sense, we get out of here. Leave these people in peace."

"Peace an' lions," I said. "We give 'em the world's worst roach problem, what we done."

"Take care of lions," Papa said, shooing me off. "Of course, of course. Don't be obvious. But after that—" and he slapped one palm across the other, "we go." He whistled.

"We must owe them something, yes?" This was Omar, sat down and now listening in. "For food, lodgings?" His face had shadows, and something tickled on my skin. I had the idea that he might have stayed up late in the night, watching Mei Shen.

"Man take care of payment," said Canelli to him.

"What man?" Omar asked.

"Black. Long hair. Ambrose, Ambrose," Papa Canelli said, working around the name as best his accent would allow.

The skin on my neck tightened.

"You know him?" I heard myself ask.

As more carnies gathered, Canelli nodded to me again in a show of disgust for my ignorance. "Of course. Been around, long time. Not lately, but. He financier." He said the word as if it existed separate from all others—a studied piece of foreign vernacular he had clearly memorized for just such an occasion. "He take care of these things."

"Frank's gonna owe big for a scrape like this." Serry leaned against the doorframe as she spoke.

Canelli shrugged with disinterest. Frank's needs were the point where his concern ended. He turned round to face the others, and made what came next seem casual and true.

"I will tell you what will happen," Papa said. "He's gonna come back and tell us we stayin' here to do a show. That we owe these bumpkins. But this a waste of time. It's bad news."

Papa had the attention of the group, and knew it. He played the moment out.

"I tell you what we oughtta do," Papa said. "We gather up what we can from what storm left, and get out!"

"And do what?" someone asked.

"Don't matter," Papa said. "This show is dead. We save ourselves."

I stopped my eyes rolling round as the words echoed. The thought hung on silence, and I wondered where Etta had got to.

TWENTY.

"Our problem's them lions," said Frank Colt.

His face was heavy. On both sides of him stood the local law.

"These men, they want the things taken down entirely," said Frank. "Of course I don't agree. I have a tranque gun so we can try to bring 'em down another way."

"Just one gun!" shouted Omar. The crowd, gathered round, rustled to itself.

"I know," said Frank. "It ain't gonna do the job on its own. Best we could hope for is to herd 'em somehow an' then get off a couple shots. That might work." More rustling.

"Do we know where they are?" someone called.

"I had track on them this morning," said Lindsay Nelson. "But they have since disappeared. I have," he continued, "Full confidence that they are still in the fields somewhere."

"Unless they made it to the backroad, where our trucks wrecked. You can't see past the trees from up here."

Not sure who said that bit. Might have been me.

"So we get lions," Papa Canelli said. "But what then? We go, yes? Leave here?"

"We'll talk about that after," Frank said.

It was afternoon by the time we were underway, as clouds gathered. About half the circus was divided into squads: Frank and some teamsters, me and Cook and Omar, the Chinese acrobats, and two other groups of carnies and police. Lindsay and his sniper rifle stood atop the house, along with a few others as extra pairs of eyes.

We went in with threshers first, and spent a good part of the morning cutting into the field from all sides about a hundred feet even—a few starting down by the far road where the wreck was, and a few up by the boarding house. We shouted as we went, banging pots and pans, hoping to cut our chances at running afoul of lions. As we worked, the locusts took flight in angry, buzzing waves. The lucky ones landed right behind us on the fresh-cut stems, but still more spun around our heads, nipping at our skin.

But this part of the process was otherwise uneventful, and within the hour we had the field trimmed and circled by men.

"Torches," Frank called out.

We lit prop torches one of the jugglers had salvaged, one for each group. Smoke floated out in sick twists of blackness in the late afternoon. I held the fire for our squad, while Omar and Cook stood by. The ink was climbing back and forth on me so bad I felt it must be something you could see, pictures sliding between my skin and muscle like insects, like they wanted me to know something but were in disagreement as to exactly what.

All around the perimeters of the field I could see the other torches go up and then come forward, licking at the nearby grasses, causing bugs to swarm around the billowing smoke. I smelled fear and gasoline, and I turned to Cook and Omar. We were gonna kill each other this way, I knew, and their faces said they knew it too.

That was when I heard the sound.

It was a klumpf, klumpf, klumpf—something soft hitting something hard, like meat on metal. It came from down the hedgerow, in the shadows where our trucks sat to wait out the slaughter. My ink started to pulse thump thump thump across my chest, keeping rhythm with that strange sound.

"You hear that?" whispered Cook. The early evening birds began to call to each other in weird koans as the sky dimmed.

"Ayuh," I said. The torches sputtered between us as I tried peering between the trees, asking for them to open. The ink sang in me in pullings and twitchings that ached, giving me no real choice.

"What you think?" asked Omar, and I could feel him getting tense.

"Burn them out!" called Frank Colt across the grasses.

I looked at the other men and shouted, "Wait!"

As the carnies looked over I slid down to the hedgerow, wishing Frank's tranque weren't all the way on the other side of that field. I made my way to the bottom of the slope under the midnight shade of trees, where the air got cooler and wetter in the green.

"Sue! Sue!" Cook was hissing through his teeth, and I turned and shushed him. He looked across the field and then hustled down to me, even as Omar had already made the decision to follow. Their faces softened to silhouette as they entered the tree line, and together we shuffled to the service road. The canopy overhead made a round, uneven light beneath. The trail was rich and the foliage velvet green, like a new snake skin.

"It's in here," Cook said.

The klumpf, klumpf kept beating its drum, but our way was blocked. The strange dirt trench stretched across the road, too deep to cross and full of soil made soft by rains. I could see again how big it was, and how purposeful—a giant cut ending in a rounded crescent. The dirt pushed outward from a central point, but it was no clearer to me what that point was than it had been the day before.

Omar stepped around the pit like it weren't there, getting to the hump of soil on the far end as best he could. Cook just stared down into the abyss, a cigarette hanging from his mouth.

With one ahead and one behind, I nimble-stepped across the dirt. The noise hummed in me now. I couldn't help but love that moment, for the beauty and stillness of the evening and the painful swell of anticipation while smoke from distant fires began to filter through the leaves. I became aware of every vibration in every tree around us, of Cook rolling the cigarette in his mouth, of the way Omar's breath echoed in his chest.

Footsteps on the path.

I spun around and raised my torch high. I saw muscles swinging like clock rotors.

Etta, Serry, and Mei Shen stood on the path, looking at me and Cook and Omar.

"What in hell?" Cook asked.

Serry held up a long-barreled airgun.

"We raided the basement," she said. "Found a horse tranque. Etta saw you running down here from the house."

"You all came for one gun?" Omar asked.

"You try waiting up at that house like old maids," Serry said.

"Women, shit," Cook said.

"One a' you fire that thing?" I asked them.

"Of course," Etta said.

Above us in the fields, the men called out. Dark bursts of movement came from the farmhouse up the hill. The light made everything silhouettes, but my ears were keen. I heard something smaller and softer, a tip-tip-tip in uneven drops, like leaves after rain.

The others heard it too. We all tensed, our eyes sliding around us. Serry's widened first, and she pointed at Omar.

I looked up at Omar's bald head. It was dotted now with brown smudges, and more appeared with each tip-tip-tip. As I watched, one ran down his temple. He reached up and rubbed it with his fingers. The smudge streaked across his cheek.

We looked at the ground around us as the spots hit the undergrowth, staining it with their rust.

And Cook was calling out in a yelp-retch, and I was looking upward. As my eyes adjusted I saw them—Misha and Rasha and Ferdinand, hung together with fat ropes, tongues hanging over their teeth, great paws loose around their sides and tails. Their intestines hung forward like drying flowers, and their eyes hung dead on me.

A piece of charred sheet metal was caught between nearby branches, and as we watched the corpses swung against it in the waning breeze.

Thump. Thump-thump.

It was a testament, or a warning. From someone with power over confused and foolish men.

TWENTY-ONE.
"There's a sickness here," Omar was murmuring. "A sickness, I tell you now."

We were soaked in blood, the stench of us rising thick like heat. The cats lay in pieces spread over the earth.

Etta had ankle-crawled out on the limb that held the beasts, and worked with fingers and knife to loosen their bonds. I got the worst of it, standing underneath to catch the corpses while Omar hauled slow on the ropes to bring them to the ground.

A small crowd of teamsters and useless deputies had gathered to watch, and their heads turned as cries echoed from across the fields. I lowered the lions to the soil, then followed the shouts to see a rounded silhouette hold something aloft. The thing wriggled and I made it out.

A lion babe, half asleep and too small to fight, hung from Papa Canelli's hands. The cub curled around his fist, its big paws swaddling the old man's callouses. It looked covered with gore, newborn. Locusts buzzed around it like a crown.

I pictured Claude the lion tamer, dead in an abandoned field somewhere, eyes skyward and not yet picked out by crows. I wondered if he might be alive, and lost like this lion child.

The meat truck that had come just that morning to take the

body of the old man now came again in late afternoon. They cleared the cats, all in pieces, and carted the slop away. With day creeping into dusk, we retired up to the house. As we walked, most were silent. Some folk focused on the lion cub, discussing what might best get it fed.

Those of us who got the lions down from the trees stopped for a hose shower along the side wall of the house. Omar spattered his head, Serry and Cook rinsed their hands, and left Etta and I to finish.

We took lye soap and scrubbed our skin of blood. I saw the pebbles pucker under her flesh and she caught me watching. I moved to overtake her. No one came to look for us.

TWENTY-TWO.

When we made it back, the carnies were gathered again in the dining room off the side of the house. The setting sun washed the room in a dim glow. Outside darkness began to crawl, and flattened the world beyond the windows. Circus folk had draped themselves over white tables like spilled food, and eyes turned toward the front of the room where Frank Colt stood.

His face was shadows, and Lindsay Nelson stood beside him.

"Law wants us in town a few more days," Frank said. "They got questions about them lions. Until the police are satisfied there's no foulness here, they asked us to stay in grabbing distance."

"Foulness hell!" someone shouted. "The lions got the old man!"

"What happened to them lions was sick," said someone else. "We oughtta tear this town apart til we find the hayseeds killed those cats!"

"You wanna run-in with some throwbacks ready to gut a lion? I'm tough, but I ain't that tough! We need to run on outta here, and quick!"

Frank raised his hands. The furor quieted.

"I know," he said. Of course he knew.

"I want to get out much as you," he said. "Put this town and its badness behind us. The old woman ran this place —"

"She gone crazy!" someone called. "They got her in hospice and she's talking to the walls, I heard."

"Her care is paid for," Colt said, "by the show's financiers. All the more reason to clear out and get to our next show."

"So what's stopping us? Is this legal? Can they really hold us here?" asked Serry.

"Yes and no," said Frank. More mumurs.

"They're not holding you individually," Lindsay said. "We did you that favor. Saved us and you a lot of paperwork, especially since a lot of you might have," he coughed, "trouble with the discrepancies between your stage identities and your street names."

He let guilt hold a moment.

"But they don't want you to leave," Lindsay continued. "It would make it a lot easier for everyone if you'll all agree to go along. Although, as we've said, any one of you is free to go."

"This is ridiculous! What are you trying to say?" demanded Papa Canelli.

"They have not held any of you," Lindsay repeated again, "But all circus equipment within town limits is now police property until they've checked it over. After that, we're free to clean it up and head on out."

Uproar rose. Frank took the room.

"This was our compromise," he said. "They have to keep up appearances just like anyone. All they know is a crew a'strangers came through and now the town's lost their boardinghouse and the folks that run it. All they want's us to stay here, answer some questions, make things square and be on our way. We should be grateful none a'this goes on the books except some downed equipment."

"We have all been through this before," Papa Canelli shouted. "Local law, no good! They make things difficult, any excuse. We stay to clean, they hold us on something else!" He stood. "We go out now, take what we need, get out this place! Leave the rest before they come back in the morning!" A cry rose. The chorus agreed.

Snarls twisted on Frank's face as the rage came up. The room was all shouting, wanting.

Etta might have grabbed my hand, but something in me took over. I stood and walked out. One sound rose over the rest as I left—the lion cub, crying for milk in someone's arms.

TWENTY-THREE.

As I walked through the downstairs, no one followed. I headed out the front door. On the steps was Mei Shen.

In the East the sky was purple and red, while the west glowed gold. She had her legs hugged up and under and she was dressed light. Her bandages peeked through. She didn't turn as I came out, just kept watching the sky darken, losing light to blue.

I thought on whether she needed company. Then I thought maybe I needed company. I sat down, brushing a few lazy hoppers away. "How you healing?" I said.

She made a noise in her mouth, considering the question. "Mm." She nodded.

"It hurts," she said. "They told me, the nurse in town, they told me sleep? But I can't. Hurts too much," she said, and looked at me and smiled to apologize for not being able to sleep in her wounds.

"I keep hearing pigs," she said. "I hear the sound they make in water, with noses. I think, how this happen? Rain, tied up, how this happen to me? I don't remember anything, just wake up, not move. But I stand, I make it out, but I have training, I think, what if I not? What if that happen? I think the people, who would do that? And do they know this, about me, that I am able to move even if my arms and legs are tied? I think of this. People, very strange."

She smiled again. "My English, you can't understand me," she said. She rubbed her wrists.

"I hear you fine," I said. "We gotta get the hell on outta here. That's what they're talkin' now, inside. I just lost patience."

She looked at me. "What you think? You think we leave? Do you know?"

She was all manners and questioning and there was something in it made me sad.

"You ask Omar," I said, picking tobacco off my tongue. "He's sufferin' through the meeting. I just had to leave."

"Mm." Mei Shen said again, and nodded with a smile. "I'll ask him."

"Right," I said.

I stood and walked to the edge of the lawn, where some of the low-level swags stood smoking. Only one of them was carny, and the other two was local boys. The carny was Frank's man Tillinger.

Tillinger was the kind of fella everyone only knew by one name. "Everyone showed up for breakdown but Tillinger, you know him." "That was a fun night last night till Tillinger puked all over the bearded lady and she socked him one."

The local boys looked like a Mutt and Jeff. Mutt was thick and Jeff was thin. Mutt and Tillinger looked like twin pitbulls, but Jeff was a sprout with hair hung over his eyes. They offered a flask before I could ask for a sip, then said they was heading to a waterhole down the road. I asked if the waterhole had cigarettes, and they laughed.

"Not a bar," Jeff said nervously. "A water hole. A pond, like. Real pretty. You'll see."

We sauntered down the hill in the direction of the hamlet, but turned off a side road. As we walked, Tillinger said he was one of the first to arrive at the boardinghouse. Jeff and Mutt had picked him up sunburnt on the side of the road and made it into town with him. Throughout the curse-filled explanation of the road he'd taken getting here, Tillinger made it clear he not only believed he'd had the worst time of anyone, but that something was owed him for it.

"All's I'm sayin' is this is shit right here," he said as we walked. "An' if no one sees that....well hell." And he drank from the bottle. "Days passing here is a deathknell for us. Even in good times, a week in the sticks means you clean that town out of whatever money they got in two, three days, max. Under our circumstances, we're in a town that doesn't want us here, and we got a lot of mouths to feed." He looked at Mutt and Jeff. "No offense to you all, mind."

"None taken," said Mutt. "This town ain't shit and we know it."

Jeff was quieter, looking at my tattoos while he walked next to me. Normally the inks got me treated lower than other men, but he watched me with a kind of envy, like the inks were a fine suit. We followed Mutt and Jeff down a dirt path between ferns and green.

The water-hole was an algae-caked mudpond with some logs nearby, and beercans all around. The air was thick with insect sounds. Locusts swarmed across swamp stones in a mass that looked like a living thing itself.

"You been all over, I bet," Jeff finally said, his eyes rolling across me. "You fight in a war or somethin'?" he asked. "You look like you did."

"Long time ago," I said. Jeff blinked with something like lust, but Mutt and Tillinger were too involved with each other to care.

"You all been out to where them trucks got smashed up?" Mutt asked Tillinger.

"Yep," said Tillinger. He hadn't.

"Shit, it's a mess out there," Mutt said. "Don't know how all that will get cleaned up. In the middle of all these goddamned locusts, too. An' some kinda big ditch out there or something! It's this weird shape, all rounded on one side. I looked at it, I said, 'How'd that even happen?' You see that?"

"We'll get it cleaned up," said Tillinger, long-suffering. "We always do." He threw a drink back. Mutt looked at me.

"You gonna help with that too?" he asked, grinning with half his teeth. "Or you just make assholes like this do it?"

"Eh, Sue's good," Tillinger said. "He ain't like most. He pitches in much as he can."

"An' the rest?" Mutt said.

"Useless," said Tillinger, and he and Mutt laughed.

Jeff still had eyes on me. "But you'll help, right?" he said, that empty stare digging in. "Y'all need to fill that hole, whatever it was."

"An' let us know what made it, you find that out," said Mutt. "All rounded out. Like a big ole shovel right in the earth! Damnedest thing."

I nodded, looked at Tillinger, who said we'd have to work on that. I slapped at the mosquitoes hovering round and begged my out, saying I needed to find cigarettes in town.

"Here's one," said Tillinger. He pulled a half-smoked joint from behind his ear, and passed it to me. I looked it over, pulled matches from my pocket and lit up.

"Head down the hill," said Mutt. "Might be something open still."

"Good luck," said Jeff, unsmiling.

I walked back the way I came, feeling heavy and rotted with a grime that had nothing to do with drink. Mutt and Jeff were men I could have been and might still be, killing space in the muck we're born in.

The last of the birds mixed with the night insects in a back-and-forth of sound as I headed west down the hill into the first little hamlet closest to the boardinghouse. Locust season had come in the late summer, when the golden parts of the evenings were longest in this country. Past some green-brown meadows and a grove of trees surrounding a water pipe that ran under the road, I entered into what passed for the neighborhood—a collection of weathered two-story houses tight together, with similar lawns and a few cars in driveways. I felt the presence of folk without seeing them, voices through one screen door, the light from a television through a window.

It didn't feel like a ghost town, despite the sleepiness of it, and I walked and smoked and supposed I'd be left alone, although I wasn't sure that was what I wanted.

Past more houses and a sidestreet, the road dipped and then arced upward. Another grove of trees hung near the top of this hill, and as the light faded the pavement beneath them had gone dark. And so it was that as I reached the dip, the shadows ahead of me released a figure with a face I recognized.

It was Mr. Ambrose, Alphonse to his friends, dressed more informally than was his usual. His topcoat hung loosely from the place where his hand met his pocket, and across his chest he wore a thin undershirt and suspenders. Even in the warm glow of evening he somehow cast a pall, but smiled his same wide smile as he approached.

"Sue," he said. "I didn't know you folk would explore the rest of town. I suppose it gets a bit antsy up by the boardinghouse?"

"You could say so," I said. "And grim. Most everyone's shell-shocked, still."

"Oh yes, the old man," he said. "An' them lions. Certainly is strange 'round here, isn't it? Like we're in God's rifle-sights."

I took a drag on my cigarette. "Ayuh," I said. "Exactly like."

"I know you've been through shit, Sue," Ambrose continued. "You know how to handle yourself. Not like some." He smiled. "Think they been around cuz they've lived carny, but that ain't real badness—still don't know what to do when somethin' bigger shows up at the door, nor even how to name it when it does. Takes a survivor to do that. I can tell you know."

My cig was already sucked down to the nub. I flicked it to the asphalt. "That so?" I asked. Ambrose arched an eyebrow and pursed his lips.

"That's so," he said. "You know what's comin' 'fore it arrives.

But you carry your smarts like dead weight, Sue. That ain't healthy. That's somethin' you'll learn—how to live with how much you understand."

I'd already run out of nothing to say. I kept looking at Ambrose. He took a glance around as he continued to speak.

"You gotta be careful, I've always felt," he said. "Bein' too smart. I'm too smart. It makes your mind wander. You make big things out of little things. You see worlds just ain't there."

He let that one hang in the air a minute, turning back to me. We sized each other a moment. Then he laughed.

"Ha! All right, I've bullshitted you long enough. I'm going to get going before daylight's gone. You be careful too—it's black as mud out here past sunset." He patted me on the shoulder, like we were friends, and went off in the direction I'd come from.

I turned. "You stayin' at the boardinghouse? Will I see you back there?"

He turned back to me and smiled. "I'll see you bright and early," he said. And he waved and turned and walked away, leaving me to watch him go.

Seeing Ambrose around made me worry an awful lot, for reasons I wasn't sure of. Which he knew, I figured—and he knew I knew, and didn't seem to care.

TWENTY-FOUR.
I continued down into the hamlet, uneasy as the sky let the light go. As I crossed into what I thought might be the center of town, there was a man out in his yard, staring off into the sad alleyways. He turned to look at me as I approached, and we each observed the other—him in hornrims and a shirt and slacks, me as I was. Beyond him I heard children, and I could see through his front screen door a few little ones thumping around inside.

He nodded as I passed and I nodded back. I wondered how it would feel if he saw me as one of them, a regular man walking down a regular street, not a thing of the hides and hollows.

It was after I was past him he called out, not loud, but enough to penetrate the evening.

"You with the circus?" he asked.

I turned and nodded, still walking.

"When's that start?" he said, a second slow, as if through smoke. I looked back at him, felt him sussing me out, but it could have been nothing. I wondered how he couldn't know the trouble our show had made in just one night in his town.

"Not sure right now," I said. "Storms this week set us back."

He nodded. "What're you doin' till then?" And he smiled, sincere and gentle.

"Holin' up, I guess," I said. "Our crew is spread all over."

He nodded again, said "Hm."

"Hey, you mind I bum?" I said, making the V of a cigarette between my fingers. He smiled, not mean.

"Sure," he said. He popped a pack out his pocket, drew one for me and even struck a match in the time it took me to put it to my mouth.

"Thanks," I said, and he nodded again.

He asked me where we came from, and I told him. Asked me how long I been on the road and I told him too. I asked him how long he'd lived here and we talked awhile. I believe he was a few years younger, and a lifetime softer. I don't remember a word we said. It was like a foreign tongue.

As we talked, we saw a figure come walking up the road toward us. Its features sharpened and I made out a man, middle aged and softer still than my new friend on the lawn. He was gray haired, dressed in shorts and a vest and hiking boots, carrying a walking stick. We both nodded to him as he approached.

He smiled to us. "Hey there!" he called. "Am I in Pickinpaw?"

"Hey there," said my friend in hornrims. "Pickinpaw's north. You're heading west."

The other man smiled bigger. "Well I know that. You all had some rain up here the other night, din'cha?"

Hornrims looked at me, then back at the man in hiking boots. "We had a storm, fella," he said. "Tore the place apart." Hornrims pointed at me. "We were just saying. He's coming through with a traveling circus show and got grounded here."

Hiking Boots looked at me with his grin quivering and his eyeballs popped. "Is that so? Just around here?"

"Up the hill toward the edge of town," I said, and pointed back the way I'd come. "All the fields tore up, and us with it."

"Where, did you say?"

I looked at him. "There's a boardinghouse up at the edge of town. Our trucks got spread to pieces all up around there. That's where."

Hiking Boots nodded, still smiling.

Hornrims looked at him flatly, and pointed a finger behind us. "And Pickinpaw is to the north. And you're heading west."

The man nodded, eyes looking up the road now. "I know that, I know that." Hornrims and I glanced at each other. "Ain't it late in the day for hiking?" he said to the Hiking Boots.

"Not hiking," said Boots, and turned back to us. "Stargazing. There's been meteor showers all over, the past three days. Don't you fellas watch the news?"

"Not really," I said.

"Never find the time," said Hornrims. I figured that explained a lot.

"I teach geology in the next county. We got a call piped through from the sheriff over here, thought they saw a meteorite come down last night," Hiking Boots explained. "Coulda been lightning if the storm was bad, but the way they said it sounded like more. You'd know if you saw it. Even a little piece would blow a sizeable hole in the ground."

"Huh," I said.

Hornrims raised his eyebrows. "Boy," he said. "Between the storm and a meteor, I'd guess we had quite some night around here."

"You sure did," said Boots. "I'm hoping I might find a crater before nightfall."

"And if you can't?"

"Well I'll just watch for tonight's meteor show after sunset. Big sky out here."

"Sure is."

My focus wandered from the men's casual speech to the town's long-shadowed streets, slashed of the last day's light.

"There a bar in this town?" I asked.

Hornrims nodded around the smoke. "'Bout three blocks down and hang a left. They close early, but it's what we got out here."

I said thanks, and told them I'd be taking my leave. Hiking Boots hadn't started moving yet, but stood transfixed looking up the hill. Hornrims sighed as I turned to go.

"Who knows," he said. "Maybe I'll join you." He looked at Hiking Boots. "In a little while."

But Boots suddenly snapped to, said "Thank you," and started walking up the hill toward the boardinghouse. Hornrims and I shrugged to each other.

His wife came out their front door with a slam that echoed on the empty streets, and joined him on the lawn. I saw her step to him. He flicked his cig out and crushed it in the grass, then kissed her head.

"Who's that?" she asked. I was walking before I heard his answer, as the shadows made dark.

TWENTY-FIVE.

Walking through town I saw no signs—no posters or flyers letting folks know a circus was coming in. Under normal circumstances a street crew drove ahead of the rest of us and set upon main streets like raiders, layering giant scrawling canvas and wheatpainted newsprint scrolls over every inch.

But here I saw nothing anywhere I looked. The town seemed vacant, just shuttered windows and flat-colored houses behind the foliage. I'd hear the low hum of a television or children indoors, but no one on the street as the last of the sun flickered from the sky.

I did as the man with the horn rims had advised, hanging a left three blocks down. This took me up thin, grassed-over railroad tracks that cut through the center of town. I walked alongside them past the first streetlamp I'd seen, into a sidestreet that glowed neon at the end.

The town bar was about what you'd expect—gray and sad and orange-gold with light. I couldn't imagine a town this small could even serve such a place, but perhaps the railroad might have brought in enough visitors, back when it ran.

I stepped into the twilight of the interior, and a thought occured that I should have worn a jacket to cover my ink. My concern dropped away as I saw the establishment's only clientele was a sad sack at one end of the bar, a broken woman at the other, and a couple silhouettes in a far corner. I took a spot midway down the barstools.

"What'll you have?" an old bartender asked.

"Whatever you got," I said.

The night was coming on, and the shadows softened. I finished my cigarette as the sad sack cleared out, followed by a swing of the front door that meant the silhouettes in the back of the room had left too.

As smoke swam around, the woman down the bar slid up on me. I could feel the heat come off her. She was maybe older than me by five years and sagged everywhere, her body in a late slow-burn, quietly suggesting what it'd be like to lose yourself in all that flesh.

She said one word. "Gin."

"Sure," I said.

She laughed. Her lips stretched from fat to thin in a half-smile. "I'm askin' if you play cards."

I thought she was kidding and told her so. She shook her head.

"I'm gonna take you to the back corner booth, and beat the hell out of you. Play for cigs and I'll steal your pack."

I looked down at the table. A pack of cigarettes was there. I turned my head sideways and the woman laughed again.

"See how nice I am? I'm even giving you a pack to start with," she said. "I'll even let you smoke one. But take the rest and follow me."

I thought of the gypsy who had once divined my future, and how that moment cast me in uncomfortable brightness.

I sat on one side of the booth. The woman dealt from the other. I asked her name and she told me, but that don't mean you need to know.

I put a cigarette in my mouth and she said, "That's your one. Rest of that pack stays on the table. They're gonna be mine."

I smiled. "You ain't even gonna fake humility?"

She smiled back. Her arched eyebrow was drawn on, the lid

underneath heavy with cosmetic.

"Honey, it's too late for that."

By the time the bartender wiped down and flipped the Open sign to Closed, my cigarettes were gone. The woman laughed on the last hand as I faked to remove my shirt.

"Ha! You keep it," she said. "Play one more for the road instead."

We began to deal while the barman walked over, pulled a chair up backward with a bottle and a glass. He plunked both on the table, and poured himself a shot.

"We dealin' you in? We'll have to switch our game," the woman said. "And I'm no good at poker."

"Hell you are, I've seen you," said the man. He had a droopy gray mustache and sheepdog eyebrows.

"Well then," the woman said to me. "Last hand?"

"I might just take a last beer instead," I said, looking to the old man. "You mind?"

"Long as I don't have to get up again," he said back.

I found a long bottle in an icebox underneath the bar, threw a few dollars on the register and came back to the table. The woman was shuffling but not dealing. I became aware of a buzzing beyond the bar windows.

"Locust season's the real thing round here," I said, cocking my head toward the outside.

"Psh," said the woman. "There's no such thing as a locust season."

"What do you call when locusts come?" the man said.

"Summer," the woman said back. The man harrumphed and turned to me.

"You in town awhile?" he said.

"I'm in the circus," I said.

"We have a circus?" he said.

"You need to read a paper," said the woman.

"Hell, I didn't know that," said the man. "What do you do in the circus?"

I tapped my shoulder while I drank. His eyes peered forward.

"He's a tattooed man, Bert," said the woman.

The old man made a long "oooooh."

"Where you from?" he said. I shrugged.

"Well, where?" he said again.

I paused. "You want the short version or the long?"

"I got nowhere to be," he said.

The woman laughed loud. He looked at her, surprised.

"What?" he asked.

"Nothin'," she said, and looked at me. "Give us the long. My daughter's got a man over. I'm not headin' home till late. You got kids of your own, Tattoo-man? That your story?"

I shrugged, and tried not to think of you.

"Can I win some cigs back?" I said.

The woman smiled, and leaned back. "If the story's good, you can."

PART 2
JUNE 23, 1983
A STORY IN A BAR

"The world is my idea; as such I present it to you. I have my own set of weights and measures and my own table for computing values. You are privileged to have yours."

- Charles Finney, *The Circus of Dr. Lao*

THE WARS.
TWENTY-SIX.
   I came home from my first war with three tattoos. This seemed a fair amount, not as much as some but enough to mark their claim on me. I'd gone in a grunt as young and dumb as any, and stumbled my way up the ranks simply because I didn't know better.
   Places where you got inked were mostly all the same. The loudest and most anxious of us would get blazing drunk and rally the rest. I was just a stroke and hadn't much started drinking. It might sound funny, but I never liked finding new ways to get pained either. As we walked through camp on the outskirts of Seoul on our first late-night drunk to get tatttooed, I asked our idea-man, a big sloppy hulk named Johnson, what it was like getting inked.
   "Like a bee sting," he said. "'Cept it just keeps goin' til you stop thinking about it."
   I told him that didn't make sense, and if it was all the same I would not be getting the anchor ringed in devils and cherubs with the words "RIGHT TO FIGHT" down my forearm with the rest of them.
   Johnson and the group stopped in our walk across the campground. He touched me light on the chest with a half-smile. "Sure you will," he said.

"I'll get inked with you," I said, "But if it gonna be a half-hour bee sting I'd just as soon get somethin' smaller."

"Naw you won't," Johnson said, and laughed. His big meat slab man-tits jiggled under his shirt.

Back then I was as reasoned as a chaplain. I don't know where I got my ease from. It disappeared with my youth.

"I'm tired enough gettin' shot to hell by day an' eaten up by slope mosquitos at night," I answered. "I don't need another reason to have trouble sleepin'."

"Tell you what," he said. "You can get somethin' small, but we get to pick it out."

"Tell you what," I said. "I'll go last, and if all y'all get through it without cryin' like women, I'll get your anchor."

The men laughed. Johnson grinned big. "The anchor and whatever we pick."

I shook my head. "How's that make sense?"

"How don't it?" Johnson's pals were lined up behind him like geese in formation.

"Hell," I said. "Last time I talk deals with a dumb mick."

TWENTY-SEVEN.

McLaren howled. Sloveki wept. Even Big Tom Styverson grit his teeth under the needle. Johnson was openly ashamed.

"This is just pitiful. Pitiful. You may be pussy but at least I didn't have to watch you cry," Johnson said, coming out from the shop. Outside I was sitting and smoking.

"Guess I'm goin' home clean then," I said.

"Hell, that's no fun," Johnson said. "Dwyer's already in the back lookin' through some books they got. Though I can't imagine anything they come up with will make you look sillier n' he did when the ink hit him and he started callin' for his mother."

"Fine," I said. "Long as it's small, I gotta special spot on my shoulder just for you."

They made me look away when I was getting it. Dwyer, this spectacled dweeb outta Ohio that wouldn't survive the year, brayed like a donkey at the tat he chose but wouldn't let me see what it was. Sloveki had me do a staring contest with him, yelling at me to keep focused on his eyes while he hooted about how much blood there was, about how my face turned red while the needle sang. The others were falling over themselves with whatever they'd chosen. As many tears as they shed getting tatted just about doubled with how funny they thought I was.

Johnson didn't laugh as much. The whole thing had gotten dumb. He wandered back outside to smoke, and said to call him when I was done.

So you know, anyone tells you the bee sting feeling goes away when you're getting drawn on is full of shit. The sound of the gun, the whine and the buzz starts hot and then creeps in deep. There's something strange about knowing your skin ain't just yours no more.

Those are the sensations that hit me quickest, and in the years since those feelings have mixed and gelled with many others. Sometimes they make me feel good and sometimes bad, and sometimes nothing.

Finally the needle's whine turned off with a thin click, and the old Chinese that inked us wiped me down. Johnson poked his head back in the doorway. McLaren and Big Tom looked at my arm.

"What in hell's that?" Big Tom said.

McLaren squinted, and then smiled like he'd found real peace.

"That," he said, "is a rabbit givin' it to a goat."

It surely was. In the space between my wrist and my elbow, a google-eyed cartoon bunny was plowing away on the backside of a billy goat, who looked just as pleased to be receiving as the bunny was to give.

It took a moment of silence as all of us peered down at it, harsh and bruised under the tattooist's lamp. Then Johnson roared. He guffawed loud and long and the others joined in, even the tattooist, like schoolboys telling fart jokes.

I looked at it, and smiled myself. It felt like a stray dog had wandered in during a rainstorm and taken up residence on my skin. It was small and just plain humiliating, but I couldn't help but be strangely pleased.

"But why's it say 'Sue'?" I said.

"Shit, you dumb fuck!" Dwyer yelled. "Who in hell's Sue? That don't make sense! I didn't tell you to draw that!"

"Fuck you!" the tattooist shouted back. "I draw picture! Picture!"

"Hell, he's right! Haw haw haw!" shouted Sloveki, holding up the tattoo book.

The drawing of cartoon sodomy in question, like most of the others from the book, was given some specificity by having its own inscription. In a faithful curve parallel to the shadow beneath the goat's rounded belly, the original artist had written "Sue" in an elegant cursive font that might, to the untrained eye, have looked like part of the larger design. And through the hand of a backwater tattooist who didn't know written English, this odd addition had, in turn, been branded onto me.

"You stupid squint! You ruined it!" Dwyer yelled, backing the tattooist into a corner. Johnson grabbed him.

"Dwyer, you idiot," he said. "You wanted a goof tattoo and you got one. Leave him alone."

"Well I ain't payin' him!" Dwyer shouted.

"You don't have to," I said, pulling out my wallet. "It ain't your tattoo."

Dwyer cursed that tattooist the whole walk back to camp, but I didn't mind. There was some small poetry in it that I appreciated. I wore the ink that whole tour, as I traveled from Seoul to the 38th parallel, and the stalemate grew. Folks started calling me Sue as I got shipped around, and I didn't mind that either. I felt less like myself the longer I was out.

I got discharged a year after. My last two pieces of mail came in the same afternoon. The first was to tell me my tour was over, and I'd be shipping out in two days' time. I was expecting that one, as most of the other boys had gotten the same thing already. The second was a telegram that my father had died.

Everyone's father dies, so I won't go into losing mine. We'd been out of touch for years. A preacher's family gets moved quite a lot as a church's needs come and go. And while it wasn't much discussed, at a certain point in my growing up it seemed easiest for everyone if my father were to travel alone, and leave my mother and the rest of us behind. We kept in touch through letters, but for a long time that was all.

On the last day before I flew home from my first war, I went back to that same Chinese tattooist and got two pieces done.

I got that goat and rabbit filled in, so as not to offend my mother. When they was done it looked like a sideways heart.

And I got a little cross, to remember my father. I wasn't much of a bible man myself, and I knew he wouldn't have cared for the gesture. It was what made sense at the time, is all. The cross is so small it's gotten lost in all the swirls of ink around it, as obscured as those rutting farm animals now covered up with blackness.

TWENTY-EIGHT.
I was on an island I didn't know the name of in the South China Sea. I was drunk. I was in an ink chair.
Laura had left me.
I met her in the southwestern backwater where I'd ended up on return from Kumsong. Hers was a town I know nothing of except my father had died there. When I showed up from hitching rides across four states, I found a community expanding and in need of men with two hands, a work ethic, and no ambitions. My own hometown had been abandoned, and what I had left felt like a grave. So I started working in a place where folks would know me by my father's name. Being close to him rooted me somehow, and that was something I needed.
I'd met Laura when we built a new gym for the school. It was a big job, one of our biggest, and the whole district came out to help. The incoming faculty, mostly bookish, would set us up a picnic lunch the days we worked. This meant a lot of pretty young things serving egg salad and chocolate cake to big dumb lugs—two kinds of folk with no business being around each other. Half our town ended up schoolteachers married to construction workers within five years. Laura and me were two of them.

Laura was blond, and tall, and whip-smart, and like me wasn't much for long discussion. We fell in love without speaking, just being round each other long enough till it was so. She was funny, and ran circles around me. I took whatever she dished, and when we were alone she said her head got light.

I won't say I was the most attentive man. Our town grew so fast that there was always new folk around. I had a taste for most anything there was to take. And I always suspected Laura, at the start of every school year, of lusting after the college-raised academic bucks that came in to teach from fall to spring. It created an obsession in me, and wondering made me mean.

One summer Laura told me we'd need to build a nursery. That changed things. I turned into the proudest foreman that town'd ever seen. All the boys from work came by, and in a week we had a room set up any baby'd be a happy piggy to live in.

That summer I got called up again.

Laura took it hard, and I felt blame in her. The army was a foreign entity. She blamed herself for marrying a grunt like me, like I was leaving on purpose for fear of being a father.

Or maybe she didn't feel that. Maybe I just thought it. It ain't nothing I can guess at anymore. But when you feel accused, you can't help but get nasty. Part of you is hungry to believe every terrible thing about yourself. You say things that make it seem like you can't wait to leave, to fall out before you're kicked out.

At least that's how I was. Maybe you're lucky. Maybe doubt don't sow such seeds in you.

I went to war again already fighting, with Laura and for her and against her, feeling like the future would empty me out, so I could be quit of her forever. We wrote back and forth, starting sweet but getting sad—both frustrated, both lonely, not knowing how to carry on.

She sent me pictures of our pink raisin. I saw her open her little eyes, stretch out her little hands. It made my highs higher, my lows unbearable. I stopped writing back. Soon the letters trickled in. Was I all right? Was I upset?

One rainy day in a disgusting port up the Mekong, surrounded by fish and aging whores, I wrote to her. I told her not to contact me. I told her I couldn't come back to her the man I was before.

I mailed that letter and then drank for half a year. I was getting schlepped all over by now, at no station more than a few weeks before another mission came down the pipe, moving us from blood and shit to blood and shit. I didn't know if I were still alive, or how I could be.

The next time I heard from Laura would be the last. Those goddamned academic bucks.

TWENTY-NINE.

It was at an army hospital when I met Johnson again.

His thickness was mostly gone, and gone fast—his skin hung loose below his neck and across his cheeks. The rest of him was wrapped in bandages, with a stump where his right hand had been. His eyes swam almost a minute before they got a bead on me.

"Shit," he said.

I smiled at him best I could without pulling stitches.

"I wanna show you something," I said.

I was sitting next to his bed on a tiny wooden cedar chair, and I scooted it forward, screeching against the linoleum. A nurse pursed her lips at me as she walked by. I was getting a lot of that by then.

I flipped my forearm over to show him an anchor, sharp as could be, with demons and cherubs flying around it. Below it was the familiar scrawl of SUE. And beneath that was a sideways heart, now filled in. Underneath that ink a rabbit railed a goat eternal.

"Didn't have the room for no other words," I said. Johnson's eyes crawled around my forearm, up my shoulder, then back down to my wrist.

Every bit was a pattern now—odd swirls that led into a

pinup girl here, a bomber there, a skull or two and stranger things. Fish and wheels and guns and shapes thrown together without plan or purpose, a maze of stories leading over the run of me.

"Fuck, man. What'd you do?" he said, his words numb with morphine drip.

"I got shot across the back a' my skull, what I done," I said, turning round to show him the wound that graced me. My hair would eventually grow over it, but for now it was a nasty worm of bunched flesh where my spine latched onto the back of my brain. The funny thing was it didn't feel like anything. It felt like space.

"Jesus," said Johnson. "You're lucky you can do more than drool an' piss yourself."

I wasn't so sure if I was lucky. There'd been shadows crept in since the shot, and I didn't know if things were more or less decent than they were before I'd gotten hit. It felt like I was being watched, and I couldn't shake the feeling.

I just shrugged.

Johnson looked at me again, seeing that my left arm had begun to crawl with pictures too, though not as many. They would all fill in. I had time.

"You been getting' those…the whole time?" he asked slow.

I'd been getting them since the drinking stopped working. There was only so much I could drink, not just when I went to bed but when I woke, and I wanted to be drunker but it didn't come. Laura was still there, and some nights she was what was getting drunk, not me, engorged on the fullness of herself. It had been a shit batch of years in a thousand dead places, through jungles hung with gutted, faceless bodies and burning towns of rotting raped corpse-women. Some days I was piles of bones and muscles and couldn't understand that it'd just be easiest to stop moving, resisting my invitation into that flat and restless world.

It had been one night in Ho Chi Minh when I lay awake

with flies licking my eyeballs and mosquitoes crawling in and out my mouth that I remembered getting tattoos with the old boys outside Seoul. I felt that first war had been part of a golden youth, now lost. Half the old boys I knew were dead, but their memories echoed.

The next morning, I'd walked into the closest ink shop I could find. The anchor tattoo was first. It was the only one I even gave instructions on. By the time we got called up someplace new I'd saved up enough money for another piece. I'd have one started in one city and finished somewhere else, so the ink itself got changed through mistranslation and a thousand buzzing pens. I came to know I could find addiction anywhere.

Soon I wasn't sure I wanted more but I kept searching, in every town and village, for some sick scared inker that would take a turn on me. I continued to feel incomplete, undone, unfinished, and the fear was rising that there might never be another way.

Sometimes I lay in the dark and looked at myself, counting the lines to remind me they were there. My skin was being shaped into something I no longer knew, and it became a higher version of itself, while the rest of me got hollowed out. I was empty eyes and missing face and mouth fallen open, hanging upide down with my guts scattered and my own blood run up my nose.

All this, in a dank hospital sitting across from Johnson on the eve of my final flight home, was more than I could say.

"Well," I said instead, looking at the painted scars covering my body. "I been gettin' them. A while now anyways."

Johnson nodded, then looked into nothing a minute. Then back at me.

"Shit, Sue," he said. "They couldn't find my hand."

And his face, all worn and jagged creases, crushed in on itself with tears.

CONEY ISLAND.
THIRTY.
Five years later, I woke with my bed on fire.
Serry shouted through my door. "Sue! Sue!" she called. "Get the hell out of bed!"
The sheets licked up from the floor to the mattress, and the wall next to me was a belching hole of flame. Smoke poured through the narrow crawlway between my building and the next on a clustered stretch of flophouses down back of the Tornado, which wasn't the Thunderbolt and wasn't the Cyclone, but still drew crowds down Neptune Avenue.
My first thought was that I had got my room lit in my sleep by way of a smoldering cigarette. As the flames tore apart my wall I realized something more had happened, something that was eating the building to ash.
Old instincts kicked in and I leapt across the room, tumbled through the door, caught myself rolling down the stairs, and flopped open on my back looking at the ceiling with the steps against my head.
Serry was kicking my shoulders, saying, "Get up, get up," and I pushed myself standing, feeling that the steps here, the wall here, was cool despite the heat above. A little scrunched man, one of the dwarves called Mr. Shift, at the bottom of the stairwell shouted to move! Move! With him was Puzzle the

Ape-Man, staring up at me through the hair over his eyes.

Serry and me ran down the stairs as something above us roared. When we hit the bottom floor cats dashed over my feet in a stream from the basement, and we followed ape and dwarf while the scaffolding caved, pushing us out into the street where fire trucks swarmed the neighborhood with bleary screams.

Winter in New York doesn't mean snow til January, so in early December all you got was cold and bite. Ice burned in the wind and I knew I would regret running outdoors in bare feet. All around folks in their underclothes poured out of buildings. On the boardwalk, the few remaining rides stood against the skyline like camp lights. We gathered beneath them while the police slammed their cars in a criss-cross to break up traffic across the crumbling corners of the peninsula.

I shouted at Serry "What is this? What is this?" as we cut through the fractured mobs, following the dwarf and the ape. Fingers were pointing up and past us and I felt something like the sun bearing down as we ran down Neptune and across 17th. We turned a corner and ran headlong into it. My eyes went blind with heat.

The Tornado was on fire.

The coaster's rails twisted upward in melted curls where the structure had cracked and collapsed. Fire hoses could do little except contain the inferno before it spread to the surrounding slums. Flames crawled across the rooftops, over and behind us from the way we'd come.

I looked to Serry, to Puzzle and Mr. Shift. They looked back at me. A crew of paramedics emerged from the fire. They rolled a stretcher between them, carrying a contorted lump of coal that used to be alive.

"Everything underneath the coaster's burnt to shit!" one man called out. "Anything else is gone. We heard this one screaming."

"Won't be screaming any more," sighed another, then: "I'll bring the wagon around."

One hand of the burned figure curled as it reached into the

air. The rest was blackened. This thing was small, not dwarf-small but close enough. Scraps of an ugly bright green pea coat peeked from beneath the ashes. I could still see the horrible mash of peacocks and pattering the fabric, and loops and repeated plumes in a checkered grid.

The coat had belonged to our old boss, Old Nan.

As we stood there, me and Serry and Puzzle and Mr. Shift looking down at her burned-out pieces, one of the tubby stagehands turned to his friend.

"Christ," he said. "Looks like the cops're rounding up everyone for questioning. I don't need that shit."

Footfalls echoed on the walk behind me. I turned around to see Serry and the dwarf and Ape-Man scrambling, cutting away and back into the crowd.

I knew bad when I saw it. The eye opened. I chased Serry through the streets.

THIRTY-ONE.
Old Nan did not live by the waterfront. She had an apartment two blocks north among the warehouses and vacant lots. I ran now through the narrow alleys and heaps of garbage, while ahead of me Serry and the others splashed through mud and the city. Even after I lost their sound, I followed.

Each of us on the show went to Old Nan's only once, after the first six months if you hadn't been fired or mangled in the wheels of the coaster. You made it that far and the other carnies would jeer you for your 'date with Nan,' and offer fair warnings that a strong stomach was needed in order to survive.

Mine had been on a Sunday afternoon in early fall, when the gray skies and rain-stained buildings mixed with the leaves that only fell purple, making the rest of the city beautiful but Coney Island a sad waste. It was the end of our season. Still, we would milk it a little longer, and if I could find work till January there was a sideshow down in St Petersburg that had an open call.

But that was some time off, so first I had my date with Nan.

She'd opened the doors and handed me a glass of wine before I stepped through, told me "Mind the cats" with instructions to dodge the shit on the floor.

"One just made a mess," she said, which I took to mean many

cats had made many messes. With the stench rising, I knew I'd be getting drunk.

Nan served tripe for our main course, while a cat Nan called Lucky took a dry, crumbly shit on the table next to me. Across the table, Nan sat and talked to me about her grandchildren, her two ex-husbands and the third deceased. She said I looked good now that I was more inked up, like she hadn't been paying attention to the new tats she'd helped pay for in the months I'd been there.

As I adjusted to her crypt's casual decay, our conversation wandered. She leaned forward and stared at me like an owl.

"You know, Sue," she said. "You're not like some."

"How's that?" I said.

"These folks are jackals, Sue," she said. "Always remember. You're dealing with animals. You never let them know where you keep your money or your housekey. I don't even keep my till at the sideshow office after dark."

"That right," I sad.

"Everything I have is in these walls, Sue," Nan said, leaning back in her chair. "No bank! No accountant! You can't trust a fuckin' one. 'Scuse me. But….you know. Lockbox in my bedroom." She patted a silver chain around her neck. "And I have the only key."

And we both howled at that, and then she swore up and down she'd kill a child at that moment for one cigarette, so I cigged her and we smoked. I stumbled home drunk and forgot most everything for weeks after.

But now, as I splashed through the alleyways between Mermaid and Neptune, I remembered pillow talk with Serry during the in-between days. Maybe I'd joked getting past old Nan's million shitting cats for her silly bedroom lockbox. Hell, maybe the joke had truth in it too.

Maybe a shadow crossed over Serry's eyes, and maybe one week later some new folks started at the show, which seemed odd so late in season. And maybe one was an ape-man and the other a dwarf, and maybe Serry had seemed to know them a bit already. Maybe them three whispered thick off by themselves some nights when I walked home.

And maybe all this flashed through my head, so neat and clean that I could not doubt. And now I ran crosstown to Old Nan's place, to prove what I already knew.

Nan's door hung open like a mouth with a broken jaw, her cats out on the front steps with flat light in their eyes as I approached. I pounded up the stairs and they scattered and headed south to mix with the cats from my own apartment building, who even now were forming tribal bands to slink through the dark parts of Coney Island.

And I entered Nan's house, sticking to the darkness like Coney Island cats, with my fur up and a low growl in me, ready to be claws and teeth when the moment struck.

THIRTY-TWO.

I got my Bowie knife nowhere specific. It had been a gift from a man whose face I don't remember, when I got called up for my first war. He showed it to to me with some sort of glee, as if the idea of cutting throats made him stiffer than any woman.

I remember the women in the mountains where I'm from. That he might choose death before sex didn't surprise me.

The knife carried no history, just some huntshop special wrapped in low-grade leather with the tag still attached. It seemed simple and unlike the mystery I thought awaited me past basic. The year and a half of my first war, the knife stayed sheathed. Perhaps I pulled it out to pop a beer, if I remembered to carry it at all.

It gathered dust most of the time I was home as well, along with the rest of my old gear. The week I got called up again, I'd been sorting through my steamer trunk while Laura avoided me in the kitchen. I found the knife, and watched it wink in the twilight of our bedroom creeping full of cold.

I'd wandered outside and found an old oak tree, then began throwing the knife against the trunk while the hardness inside me began to breathe. I threw until I couldn't see, until the dusk had turned to dark. When I packed for true I made sure the knife was in my bag.

It was my second war that I began collecting operating tools. So did every man, although they wouldn't tell you. Knives and blunts and bits of hurt I found in one village or another. For every bit of ink on me, I did things to feed those long strange years.

I hadn't even realized till I got running across the neighborhood toward Nan's, but somehow that mountain huntshop Bowie knife had made it to my hand when I began chasing Serry through sidestreets. It might not have been till I crept down Old Nan's front hall that I felt it in my fist clutched reverse, teeth out, while my other hand reached into the dark.

It may not have been till I heard sounds of movement that I felt my grip tense round the hilt, and not till I was running across the apartment that I felt the old stirrings. Then I was in Nan's room.

The room was hung with floral paper withering from the walls, photographs, and framed crochet. A lockbox sat on the bed, and the dwarf named Mr. Shift stood above it with a hammer meant to break it open. His eyes swung up to squint at me, while another shape rushed forward.

I slammed the ape-man Puzzle in what I believed to be his guts. This was something I could do, back then, when the training hadn't fully left me.

Puzzle doubled over, vomiting into his pelt. I kicked him in the face and head. Serry was shouting somewhere. I looked up and the lockbox was gone and dwarf legs hung out the bedroom window. I realized Serry shouted not at me but Shift, about to scamper off with the spoils.

I crossed the room to grab him back, but misjudged his weight and wound up getting pulled through with him, falling outside into garbage. Shift was already up and running past me, but I rolled on him, pushing him to the ground.

He spat tobacco juice and mucus, but I'd had worse. I held the knife to him and he sneered. The street light revealed weird scars across on his face from many knives that had come before.

"What've you done?" I said, grabbing round his neck to keep him.

"We'll cut you in!" he said. "Lemme up, we'll cut in you in for nothing!"

"You lit her up, you little shit!"

"So what?" Shift spat. "What do you care?"

"She did nothin' to you," I said. "Nothin' to you and now she's gone."

That's what I think I said. Perhaps I only hit him, over and over.

"You don't know shit," he whispered through bleeding teeth, an eye weeping down his cheek. "That place was due for torching. Nothin' in it worth keeping."

"Worth a lot more than what was in that old woman's lockbox," I said.

He shook his head like I was stupid

"That's what you think this was? Over a lockbox? You're an idiot." He grinned. "You got no idea. You know how much that property's worth? How much we got paid to torch it? Stealing the lockbox was just a put-on. That show was dead." He grinned. "Except to trash like you."

I felt blind hate. I had no room in me for him. The Bowie hung above his eye.

THIRTY-THREE.
Serry stood at the mouth of the alley as I came out. I handed her the lockbox. It was warped shut from where I'd bashed in Shift's skull.
"You keep that," I said.
Serry looked at it, then back at me.
"I'm sorry, Sue," she said.
"You wanna explain this to me?" I said.
She looked at her feet, and up again.
"It was good money."
We took separate sidestreets, and neither she nor I looked back. Only darkness saw us leave.

MAUREEN.
THIRTY-FOUR.

I will tell you one more thing. I was crossing America drunk, or at least part of it, which may have been halfway through Ohio or Tennessee. I got a long way just stumbling, stumbling, carrying a bottle and pissing in my clothes. It was how I had escaped New York, and those I thought might be after me for the death of Mr. Shift. I didn't know if anyone cared who I was anymore. I settled into a haze for months after.

I found myself on a dirt road, much like the one where I'd be stranded years later when my circus got grounded by a storm. And on this evening as I stumbled, half-running and half-hobbling, hiccupping and crying to myself, another storm was coming, making the air hot and purple-yellow like a bruise, while the sky lanced quiet with lightning far away. I could smell rain and it had me in some kind of panic, as if in escaping it I might outrun some horror inside myself.

I had seen a house with no barrier for wind nor rain, but solid against the last streaks of dusk. I saw it like a beacon on that darkened evening in midsummer when the world had lost meaning. My shoes were stolen somewhere east and my feet no longer felt the gravel.

I don't know when I collapsed, but it rained and I slept in rain like a blanket.

THIRTY-FIVE.
Strong hands lifted me, bringing me into light, throwing me across a large pine table so I groaned as my body hit the wood. Soft voices said that there was little else to do but keep me from the storm.

A light hung over me, rocking from tumult. My neck ached, spine ached, all twisted as I lay on my stomach, cheekbone pressed hard on pine. One hand attempted to push me up and I think it was my own, crawling backward, the other arm assisting, while the fog thinned. A rocker was creaking above the white squall, and I smelled the stink of drool dried down my face. Welts and wounds woke up with me.

I saw the blue wisp of cigar smoke before I smelled its odor. A body sat against a window dripping with the last of the storm. I put my hands to my face and pushed the blood into it with my fingers, begging the rest to just wake up.

When I could sit up, I did. I saw two women, one young, one older. The older smoked at me from a chair, while the younger leaned in a doorway. Beyond them a wood stove burned.

"'Lo," I said.

"'Lo," the older woman said. Cynical, half warm. Like you'd be.

"How you feel?" she said.

"Could I get some water?" I said.

The younger woman moved to the sink and poured out a cup, then passed it to me.

"Thank you," I said to her, then drank. When it was gone I looked at the women again.

"I'm sorry," I said. I didn't know what for, only that it seemed right saying it.

The woman in the chair had one hand resting on the barrel of a rifle. She looked at me, dragged on the cigar clamped in her mouth, then blew out.

"Yeah," she said. "I bet you are."

THIRTY-SIX.
The elder woman was a painter. She called herself Maureen. The younger woman was her daughter Kate, and she attended to the day-to-day. I didn't find her sullen, but peculiar, a last seed on a dandelion, clinging on by short hairs but not able yet to blow away.

I stayed three days, till the storm was gone and it seemed safe to travel. By day I helped with chores while Maureen painted in her studio. In the evenings time was mine, and the second night after supper Kate and I smoked among the hay bales one field over while the sun set.

"I don't see myself here forever," she said, dragging on a cig I'd rolled. "These are good," she said, watching smoke curl up. "I'm gonna save up and move, but—" and she nodded over her shoulder, "—but she needs me."

Neither asked what I was doing, or how I came to end up drunk in their front lawn. Whatever story I might tell wouldn't clear up anything they couldn't well assume. I offered up some excuse that first night, after I'd bathed and borrowed a clean shirt. I suggested something vague about being in a bad way, with a fever that had plagued me since the winter's thaw. Maureen offered that more could be said once I was feeling better, a conversation that never came.

There was a knowing of how things were. Badness all blends, given time.

On the last night, early after dark, we sat round in Maureen's studio. I looked through her canvases while Kate watched out the window at the light disappearing. Maureen puttered at an easel, discontented.

"Tattoo man," she said to me, blowing smoke. "You gonna look for more circus work, when you leave here? Is that your plan?"

"No ma'am," I said. "I'm done with that awhile. I'll look for labor work, I guess. Don't know where."

"Too bad," said Maureen. "Waste of all that art got done on you. Except those empty patches. What are those about?"

I looked at the places where my skin poked through—one across my sternum, and uneven spots high on either shoulder. There was a fourth below the back of my neck that I couldn't see.

"I suppose I just ain't got to 'em," I said. "Seems easier to wait 'till something strikes me."

"That's your problem, Sue," Maureen said. "That is exactly it."

And she laughed in a crow's cackle. "C'mere," she said. She slapped a wooden chair next to her at the easel, then beckoned to me with one finger.

I sat down. "Take off your shirt," she instructed.

Across the room something flickered across Kate's eyes, but just as soon was gone.

Maureen wiped down the blank spot on my chest with a rag. Several jars of muck were lined up behind her easel, clotted with half-mixed clays. She dabbed a brush in one, then looked at me. "I'm gonna need you to hold still," she said.

I gestured toward the brush. "That ain't exactly how the rest of these were done," I said.

"At the rate you bathe, this'll last long enough to stain you," she said. "And I want to do it. Never tried a man as a canvas, and here you are. I see you and I must paint, so let me do what I'm meant to."

Maureen went to work on the center of my chest, painting something I couldn't see.

"You know why we don't ask you about yourself, Sue?" she said.

"Politeness, maybe," I said back.

Kate spoke. "You talked," she said. "That first night, you talked."

I looked at Maureen, who nodded to tell me it was true.

"You called for several folks," she said, and dabbed at me again. "For someone to come back to you, for someone to let you go. You told someone you'd never meet them. You told someone you were sorry. That you were wrong to leave."

"Four different people, Sue," she said. "Four clean spaces on your skin."

Maureen looked at me. "I'm filling all them in for you, so sit back. We were always meant to meet this way."

I sat back, trying not to think what led me to this place, a cool tingling running through me. I felt the bristles rasp across my chest, smelled oils mix with evening and the wood walls of that room. I watched the dust swim out the window, through the low shimmer of evening heat. A thin trail of smoke slowed as it left Kate's cigarette, then stopped. I had the sensation of time fixed.

Sometimes my mind wanders back to this moment in the nighttimes, when the eye is closed and I have quiet. I live in the stalled future of that still block of space, brushes whispering on my skin, and can only wait.

THIRTY-SEVEN.

It was a small wagon floated in disease. I sat at one end of a table hung with tapestries. It smelled of incense and dead things.

The old gypsy was a witch, or perhaps the other way around. She was older than Old Nan had been, and tougher by far than Maureen. I watched her as she checked on her tea, cloaked in dark veils, while I felt like I was steaming in the heat. She reeked of waste. She asked me questions about my travels, my life, as if I were on trial. I can't remember her accent, just the click of syllables as she peeled pieces off me.

"Your tattoos are interesting," she said. Her words felt circular. "So many layers, and time. Do you have a favorite?" She sipped tea.

"Can't say," I said, breathing through my mouth.

"Can't say, but there is," she said. "You're aware of their pattern?"

A fly buzzed my ear. "Not sure what you mean," I said.

Her eyes peered so hard I swore they floated.

"Don't know?" she said. "Is that true?"

The way she spoke cut through me so I wasn't sure if just by speaking she changed the shape of what I knew.

"If you truly got those tattoos unplanned, over years, which I would guess you did," she said, "that's passing strange."

She looked at me again. "And then here you are with me. That's strange too."

"What's so strange about it?" I said.

She lifted her spoon from her cup, sucked it clean. "We do fake and shimsham here," she said, "With men smarter than you. Then here's real magic, and you don't know a thing." She waved a hand over me. I held my gaze. She blinked twice.

Reaching behind her, the witch pulled down one stinking tarp from the wall. As the sheet fell, it revealed a larger shelf of leather books, teeming with must.

"What do you see?" she asked me.

"Books," I said. She sighed.

"Books," she said. "At least a hundred of them. Maybe more. Too much for one old lady in a horsecart, that's sure."

She pulled one dank volume from the shelf and blew across it. Dust wafted.

"Now you and I could sit here with these books," she said. "And I could show you a book about ley lines and a book about palmistry. I could show you star charts and jewish mysticism and all sorts of things. But I just don't know how much it would mean to you, and I am tired."

She sighed, and leaned back in her chair. "A man walks in with tattoos that form a pattern he doesn't understand, and asks me to explain. And I can't explain. No matter how you got those tattoos. It's not important anymore. It's the skin that keeps you safe," she said. "Or ignorant, which is close. They will call to you. If they have not already. The skin will let you know it's there."

There was a long quiet. I cleared my throat. "So does that mean I have the job?"

"Of course you have it," she sneered. "Don't insult me. You knew you did when you walked in. You know you've got something. You just don't know when you got it, or how long it will stay." She pointed her spoon sharp at me and glared. "I know what kind of dumb you are, and what kind you aren't. Now get out."

And I left her, burst out into sunshine at the center of a crowd of circus folk—my first true circus, up from Coney and every dog-and-pony since. I'd trailed every traveling show through the square states, following whim and rumor, a man looking to be new. For the first time in a long while I felt unfollowed by night and shadow.

I'd started in the next city past Maureen's, with the marks she'd painted on me still splattered there. I found an ink shop, plunked down money and said I'd do whatever needed to pay the rest, if one of their ink men would make the fading paintings on me permanent.

The owner looked me over. "You look strong," he said.

"Been said I was."

He smiled. "I get five men a week in here, no money, sayin' they'll work for ink. I turn 'em all away. You, though. You." He stared a while. "I gotta roof needs fixin', a few other things done too. You do that, I'll get you squared. I'll do traces of that art right now, before we lose it."

"'Spose I'll be able to take a bath after," I said. "Which suits me fine."

Roof took a week, and after that the man gave me my inks. Did it fast and I bit through it. When he was done we both stood at the mirror.

"Still don't know what they is," he said, running fingers over his moustache.

"Me neither," I said. "But they look good. Flowers? Is that what?"

"Thought it might be flames," he said. "Ugly. But they look good."

Each moment felt placed. The tattooist sat along a road I'd got lost down. I walked north that night to find a job. As I walked through the evening I felt different. Sharper then I had in years, and clean. No cloud hung over me. The world felt born new.

Two days later, I found a traveling show needing an illustrated man. That's when I was sent to interview with the circus gypsy. And as she said, I knew before I interviewed that I already I had the job.

"They'll know," she whispered to me in the days that followed. I didn't have the most tattoos she'd ever seen, she said, nor the prettiest. "But the marks will know there's something in your skin. That's why you're hired. Something's stained on you, more than just the ink. That's what they'll believe."

Winter killed the gypsy. She'd been an old woman, after all. It was later, once I'd started and was getting to know the crew—Cook, Omar, the Simple Twins, plus Frank and his woman Etta—that was when the letter came.

We didn't much get mail, of course, except at Western Unions in the bigger towns where folks that cared might know we'd be. My folks were dead, which made it odd when one of the dwarves dropped off an envelope to me in my trailer late one night. "Came in yesterday," he said. "Half of us don't know your name, so it took awhile to get around."

It was small and frail and yellowed and I opened it, smelling cigars and ash. A single sheet fell out. I sat on the floor and began to read.

Sue.

An old beau of mine rang tonight to say he'd been to the circus. He lives to the north and west but not too far. I asked him if the circus had a tattooed man. He said as a matter of fact there had been, with odd shapes on his chest and shoulders. I knew it would be you.

First, I'm glad you got the work, Sue, and that it's a job where you can show off what's been toiled so long on. And I'm touched because I think this means you got my paintings inked. You did it without me ever explaining what it was they were. I suppose that was a small cruelty on my part.

Now that you're unlikely to come back and rail at me, I want to let you know what it is that's on your skin. I think once I tell you, you won't unsee it, but you can still rest satisfied that to the world they'll just be shapes and whorls.

I told you that when you first arrived, you'd called out in your sleep. Do you remember? I can't tell you how I knew who these four people were. I'm just an old woman, who's lived a long time.

On your left shoulder and your right are hands. One pair is your fathers'. One your mothers'. One who left you, one who wouldn't let you go. So it is everyone, Sue, those cursed with knowing them who birthed us. For those that don't it's no less sad, so don't think too hard on the lot God gave you.

On your back are eyes. If I could, I'd cleanse your heart of the person you're sorry to. Probably a woman or a man that did just as much to hurt you as you may have done to them. But guilt and sorrow are what kills us, and the hurt you carry is a wolf scratching at your door. I put its eyes at your back, Sue, so that nasty wolf might be always be turned away and distracted by something else. It's the best I could do for you, since I can't cure you of the hurt you hold to.

The ink on your chest is what I feel worst about. When you landed on our table that night we cleaned your pockets, to try and find out who you were. Kate found one small picture, almost faded and washed out. I never told you we had seen it, and we put it back before you woke. But I thought on it a long time. And in your sleep you cried out, saying, "I'll never meet you," and in my heart I knew who it was and what you cried for.

On your chest your daughter sits, Sue. She's curled and small and sleeping, and I promise she's content. I can't give you any more than that, nor do I know if there's some real small girl out there who's calm and happy in her heart. These aren't about the people, Sue. It's about the versions of them you carry with you. It's about making peace with ghosts and guilt, and I hope it's something you can do.

But I'm just a strange old woman, painting scenes on wanderers, writing letters so in my own way I might make peace with tensions I can't assuage. If this finds you, I hope

you'll forgive me. I wanted only to make you whole.
M.

In the silence of the circus car I felt a creeping, a whispering on my skin. Like feathers, then insects, squirming, crawling, climbing.

It was the inks. They were stretching. They were scratching. As Maureen's letter shook between my fingers, the inks, like curses, skittered themselves awake.

I twisted. I writhed. I swore. But all that came much later. For the first minutes, there was only horror and quiet.

Perhaps what Maureen sought was pure, but what she believed about ghosts was wrong. The past weighs us, and we're beholden. Those of us who try to find ourselves by patterning our skin are pulled forward and back at once. I carry memories with me. The marks have become a prison too.

It was then I understood, as I have since, exactly what the witch had meant. The ink lived in me, all right. It poured from the black pupil of the eye that hung above me, that had never left. No matter how many doors I opened, there weren't rooms in me enough to hold it all.

THE WALK HOME.
THIRTY-EIGHT.
The bar was quiet. The cigarettes were butts and ash.

The story I've told here isn't perhaps the one I told then, sitting in a small town south of Pickinpaw. But it was close, excepting those parts that might have got me in more trouble than the story's worth.

The old man, buried beneath his eyebrows, stared low at the table. The woman made her smoke last, blowing it over our heads. Silence cleared the space around us. The man looked up.

"So," he said. "Where's it you said you was from?"

The woman smiled. I crushed my butt.

"I didn't," I said. "Mountain country. East."

"East," the man said. "That makes sense."

The woman crushed her butt too, then stood, grabbed a trash bin near our table and swept the mess away. The old man watched, tired and dumb, till she put a hand on his shoulder and he sat up with a start.

"Bedtime, Bert," she said. "Big day tomorrow."

"That's right," he said. "Big day of the same shit."

The woman crossed to the door and turned to me. "You too," she said. "Walk a girl home?"

I shook hands with Bert and then we left. Behind us I heard him lock the door and ramble off inside, wherever it is that old men go when the world's forgotten them.

"Some story," the woman said, as we stepped into the run-down street. She looked at me, squinting half her eyes. "That all true?" she said.

"Most of it," I said. "The rest I just made up."

"It's a good one," she said, nodding.

"Thanks," I said. "I'll remember that the next time I tell it wrong."

We walked down the railroad tracks, feet crunching gravel in heavy pairs. She talked to me about her daughter. "Hope I don't walk in on her and her boyfriend," she said. "Hell, this's the latest I been out in twenty years."

Then she stopped, looking down a gray alley full of doors to tiny bungalows.

"That you down there?" I said. "Still need an escort?"

"Think I can make it fine," she said. "Hell, can't have you knowin' exactly where to find me, can I? You carnies steal kiddies in their sleep."

"And worse," I said. "Can't fault you there."

She stuck a hand out. "Good to meet you, tattoo man," she said.

"Thanks, hometown girl," I said, and shook. "Keep a light on."

She grabbed my hand and brought me close, then smiled warm. "You know I will. We always do." Gave my hand a squeeze, and let me go. "Take care of yourself," she said, and walked off into the darkness of the alley. Then she turned back and smiled.

"Look away!" she called. "Can't have you know where I'm going!"

I smiled, and headed back the way I came. Up the hill, out of town, walking slow, hoping the spell of the evening wouldn't leave soon.

THIRTY-NINE.

By the time I reached the boardinghouse it was dark. The nightbirds called to each other in the trees, and the locusts rose in unpatternable waves. I hadn't told them folks in town the worst bits, the bits I told you. I changed and obscured those parts so only the tone survived. Maybe that made it worse. My own shadow, dim though it was beneath the moon, sucked me deep into each step. Up the road the boardinghouse sat against a low blue-black sky. Stars were hard to come by except where the clouds broke and they glistened icy flat.

I saw a blackness that shouldn't be there on the porch as I walked up. Closer to it, I made out Frank Colt, but he seemed unaware, immobile. His chin sunk into his chest, and he watched me come beneath half-lidded eyes. He made no movement to me, and I thought he might be drunk and gone.

I touched a foot down on the first step and his hand went out like the arm of a crane swinging. He grabbed at my jeans, squeezing and releasing.

"We're gonna stay," he slurred. "We're stayin'. We're stayin."

He patted me and looked off into town.

"All right," I said. I stepped past Frank, thinking all his energy was spent.

"Didn't wanner go," he said. I turned back to him. He was a

silhouette in the dark.

"What d'ya mean ?" I said.

He looked back around. His eyes were shining. He shook his head. Looked away again.

"Nope," he said. "We shouldn't stay. Should..." and he pointed off toward town, and past it. "Get the fuck out of here," he finished.

"So you're in charge. What's stopping us from going?" I asked.

"No one," he said, his mustache swimming across his face. "Ambrose convinced 'em we oughtta stay. Make ... a little money. Make ... nice with the townfolk. Appease the local law. Maybe find out who got the lions." Frank shook his head. "Whatever that's worth."

"But you're the boss," I said. "Just tell 'em we all have to leave, if no one can hold us here."

He looked back at me and sneered. "You think that's how it works? Hell." His words came together slow.

"I'm thirty-nine, Sue. You ever met a man owns a circus at thirty-nine? I'm the youngest ringmaster you'll meet in your lifetime. And I've owned this thing seven years. Seven years! Hell, I started out packin' dynamite for the human cannonball. Not for the cannon, you know. But..." he paused, looking for words. "...the pyrotechnics. When that boy got out, I made him look good." He pushed on each syllable. "People think I ain't earned what I got now. They don't know. I worked hard and then some. And even so, I paid a price."

He paused again. His face was dark. "I paid a price. And there's somethin' I know," he said. His eyes swung back up to me. "You can't make these folk do anything. I couldn't have made them leave. Gotta hold the middle ground. Hell, I wish they'd thrown a coup, up and left already! Thought they would."

He sighed. "But we're stayin'."

"Well," I said. "One way or another, sure it'll be fine. What's three more days, anyway?"

But there was something slow creeping into Frank's voice,

and the air around us. I was trying to leave because I was run down, and sad and tired. But I also had this itching feeling. I didn't want to know what was running through Frank's mind.

Frank was shaking his head, slow, slow, and he whispered, "No. No, ain't gone be fine."

I don't know what it was I saw in him, but I sat down.

"All right, Frank," I said. "Why ain't it gonna be fine?"

"We need to leave this place," he said, his lip trembling. "It's bad here."

It was the second time he'd been on the verge of breaking before me in as many days, and I didn't know what to make of it. Before this I never had to deal with him. I thought of Etta. No good could come.

"Hell, Frank, we all know it's bad," I said. "Our trucks is wrecked, what happened to the lions. Some old coot got killed we don't know from Adam. I hear you. We should go. Just tell 'em what's what. Screw Ambrose. Let's cut our losses."

But Frank was pushing his head back and forth, dripping with drinker's sweat. "We're gonna stay," he said. "We're gonna stay. We're gonna eat ourselves alive."

"Frank," I said. "Don't get like that, nothin' has to be. I know it seems—"

Frank stopped me.

"We have a buyer, Sue," he said. "He's been trailin' us all season, checkin' our numbers, closin' in to snatch us up. He knows how much money our show turns over, and he's gonna make me an' offer. And that offer's gonna be right. He's gonna tell me this show's cursed, and with everything that's happened in this town. We won't get no shows as long as my name's on the banner."

He looked at me. "And he'll be right, Sue. Word gets around what happened here, we won't be able to book nowhere. You all think a circus keeps to itself. None of the bad gets out. But you're wrong. A man's dead. Our lions is dead. That ain't normal bad, Sue. That ain't something can be contained."

He looked into his chest again. "We have to move to stay ahead of the buyer, Sue. The sooner he gets here and offers me what I know he will, the sooner I'm gonna cave. All that keeps me goin' is stayin' on the road. I'm not so strong to turn down a good offer." He sighed. "I never was."

"Christ, Frank," I said. "You can't sell out mid-season. Folks is away from their homes for this. You can't send them packing before the fall comes."

"It don't matter," Frank said. "It don't matter. I've known this would happen."

"What's that mean?" I asked. "Is it that Ambrose fella? He your buyer? Is that what all this is?"

Frank sniffed. "Naw," he said. "He's just a man."

"So what?" I said. "You got us sold out to the devil? What is it, then?"

Frank paused again, the longest one. The silence stretched a year.

"Might as well be," he said.

He looked at me again. His eyes were hollowed out.

"Might as well be."

I walked up the steps and tripped over something on the stoop. I bent down and picked it up. It was a small leather journal, the pages scrawled with thick-lined handwriting.

"Dropped this," I said to Frank. He took it from me.

"Penny for my thoughts?" he said. "Mine ain't worth shit."

My skin shivered. His pages had been packed with letters, but all jumbled. They made no sense at all.

FORTY.

I won't tell you that I left Frank then.

I won't tell you that I stumbled up the stairs of that old house, enfolded in death, to the tiny back room I'd stolen from a corpse.

I won't tell you Serry's body waited for me. I won't tell you I collapsed there in her arms, like punishment.

PART 3
JUNE 24-26, 1983
THE BIG TOP

"The Illustrated Man, stripped to the waist, all nightmare viper, sabertooth, libidinous ape, clotted vulture, all salmon-sulphur sky rose up with annunciations:
"The last free event this evening! Come one! Come all!"

- Ray Bradbury, *Something Wicked This Way Comes*

FRIDAY.
FORTY-ONE.

Hailstones banged down on windows and shutters, gray specks on a flat gray sky. The light cast a glare in our little attic-room, illuminating the filth in that unkempt space.

Serry was buried in her own hair when I woke, dead gone. I rose and stretched like my skin was full of insects, rubbing my face, grabbing what clothes I had. The crack of a larger stone hit the window as I stepped into the hall and I saw Serry twitch, so I moved before she could look to see me go. I felt jangled, like I was eggshells strung together in bad shapes. I was cold and needed bathing and a lot of other things.

I walked down the halls of this crooked house. It seemed like things had changed in the night, with angles and floorboards twisted in passages no one used or went to anymore.

I imagined the old woman and her dead husband living here alone, the place empty from winter through the spring, both moving in separate circles amidst hot soup lunches and afternoons spent napping. It seemed cozy and the saddest thing.

A small step at the end of this hallway led into another, an adjoining branch painted green. The two hallways were connected strangely, and I felt again this house had been hackjawed from roaming disparate parts, like trees grown together in a forest. I thought of marriage trees that stood alone in a field near my childhood home, but I wasn't sure if I placed them right—if they'd been borne from that memory or another field in another time, slicked with rain and muck in the decades I'd lost track of them.

I stepped onto the landing of the passage, the floor creaking. It was cleaner and brighter, and I looked back at the dingy hallway behind me. Standing here, it looked as though the other hall fit all wrong. Once in one hall, the counterpart would always feel off and put together backwards.

Here, I felt heat come up from the kitchen. A wardrobe stood here, and I opened one door to find quilts there for taking. I wrapped one around me, and the clutch of home in it wrapped itself around me too.

Above me was a pitter-patter, and I looked up to see a skylight cut into the house's roof. Through it, a slush of hailstones dropped and burst. I breathed in the cooking smells, the wood smells, the house smells, like I could claim them.

"What you doing?" Serry was standing at the lip of the hall, her hair a swarm, in skivvies and an undershirt with her belly peeking out.

"Not sure yet," I said.

"Make a little room?" she asked, and crossed to me and pulled my arms apart, shuffling my shoulders round her own. She looked soft, waked-up and earthly. I felt a layer of things, a slow numbness from the places where we touched.

I stepped back from her, mumbled something, and turned to go downstairs. She didn't follow.

FORTY-TWO.

Outside, hail had peppered the land so thick it looked like an early frost. The front foyer was a mess of blankets and makeshift beds, sacked out with clowns and dwarves and skydancers in a chorus of snores. It seemed our band had free reign of the house now. There was no one left to stop us.

Food smells wafted from the back of the house. As I looked through the maze of bodies, Cook stepped out from the kitchen down the hall. He was drinking coffee from a tin cup from the camp kitchen, despite probably having a cupboard full of other choices. He looked like stink and flies. But he nodded to and waved me toward him, his face serious. I stepped around Yang Tsin and the Flying Dutchmen, then followed.

"Shit, Cook," I said as I came into the kitchen. "What the hell?"

Steel bins of food were out and scattered. Not just one pot but several were on different burners of different stoves, and I didn't see one bean anywhere.

"Sit," he said, and pointed at a stool. He walked to a stove with that same weird saunter he always had, the cigarette hanging from his mouth. He picked up a pair of spatulas and scraped across the skillets, then slid me a plate: eggs, bacon, potatoes.

"Hell, Cook," I said. "You got skills after all."

Cook was sat on a stool next to a small window by the farthest stove, looking at the world outside. He took a drag and blew out.

"There's more," he said. "And coffee."

The food on my plate was already gone. I poured myself a cup, took another piece of bacon and sat back down. The coffee steamed my face and I watched my own reflection in its surface, collecting the parts of me went missing in the night.

"We the only ones awake?" I said.

"Nope," Cook said, stretching. "The old lady who owns the place took sick and's staying at the next farm. Wimmin went over across the fields to see her. An' Frank an' that ol' fuck Lindsay Nelson went down to the county clerk to set up permits for tomorrow night. They're already back and in their beds, I think," Cook said.

"Tomorrow night?" I said. "So the show goes up?"

"Yep," he said. "Gonna search all the fields for pieces of scrap, put together some kinda thing. Think it might be the last one, too. You know." He nodded, blew out. "What I hear."

"That so," I said.

"I'll tell you who's gonna be pissed," said Cook. "Canelli. All his little family." He wiggled his fingers. "They wanna leave. Don't wanna do even one more show. Hell, I'd go."

"Oh?" I said.

"Sure!" he said. "Where the hell are we, out here? Just get out, move on. But whadda I know. Just gotta go along."

"That's funny," I said. "Frank said the same thing about you all."

Cook looked at me. "Huh," he said.

We both heard shuffles in the hall behind us, and as we turned Frank Colt and Lindsay Nelson walked in.

Frank looked like he'd lost a pint of blood and been sucker-punched by God. He'd passed out in his clothes from the night before. His suspenders hung off his belt and undershirt was sweat-stained. His eyes were purple and his cheeks were pale.

Lindsay's skin was rosy. He looked well-slept and ready for fisticuffs with a rabid bull. He wore a downy bathrobe and came in with "Morning, Sue," walked to the stove, and began his own meal. "Cofffee, hmm! Bacon, hash browns, oh, and eggs . . ."

I thought it might be a miracle if Frank could even pour himself a cup. But he did, and leaned against the counter, drinking it slow with his hair around his eyes.

"Mornin'," I said back to Lindsay. "Mornin', Frank."

"Mmm," he said.

"Did you hear, Sue?" asked Lindsay Neslon. "Your permits are all set. The show goes up tomorrow night!"

"I heard," I said. "What kinda show this gonna be?"

Frank shook his head behind his coffee cup, but Lindsay answered.

"We've gotten some men from town, along with our boys, to scout for lumber as well as anything we can salvage in the surrounding fields," Lindsay said. "It'll be stripped down—bare bone! But authentic! Real honest stuff!"

"Hmm," I said. Frank dropped the cup from his face.

"Don't worry, Sue," he said. "I'll figger somethin' easy. Sideshows shouldn't have trouble. Y'all won't notice it. We'll talk tonight."

The room was twice as small with these men in it. I spied some old farmcoats next to the sink.

"Think I'll go for a walk," I said.

"I'll go with you," Cook said, just as quick.

FORTY-THREE.

Pale whiteness infected the air, making it soft and still. The morning hail was dying off in stutters. It fell against leaves that had been knocked to the ground in the storm, on green grass in a layer of seasons. Near the horizon the haze ate the world.

Cook nodded to me. "The women's thisaway," he said. He headed in the direction of town, walking along the treeline above the road that dipped into the hamlets where the houses sat. Here a path tracked inward, and the land opened into a yellow-green grid of broken stalks and long grasses. It looked to have been a wheat field at one point in its life. We followed the path to a dirt trail, the trees on either side trapping the stillness. My feet crunched in hail and frosted grass.

The farm coats I'd grabbed cut down on the wet chill. For a moment I could imagine me and Cook as men who had only ever known this place, who walked in farmclothes through forests as a matter of course. The weird ritual magic caused by circusing, the magic we never noticed till it was gone, seemed now to disappear, leaving us alone in gray backwoods.

"You're right," said Cook suddenly while we walked. "I should just leave. Weren't always no Cook, you know. Just ended up that way."

"Huh," I said.

"When I was young I helped my mother more'n my father with chores and such," Cook said. "Always when t'other boys was out with stickball or helpin' build a shed, I was makin' pies. Weren't till I got older I started thinking I might be a cook. My mother died. Had a lump got hard. That's what killed her."

Cook's eyes watched the ground as we walked.

"I found my mother's recipes in a little tin. I lit a cigarette on the stove and smoked a hole right through 'em. My father came home and found me. He beat me till there was blood on the kitchen floor. When I come to, I bought a black pickup and drove to Chicago. Found a dishwasher job, till they saw I could fry an egg."

Above us, a bird crested on chill wind, then screamed and plummeted past the treeline.

"A girl come through the downtown spot where I worked," Cook said. "She had sparkles round her eyes. She didn't say much. But there was somethin' in her. She was circus. That night I ran off with her when we closed. We shacked up awhile."

Cook was carrying a stick while he walked, thrumming it against tree trunks. As quick as he'd started talking, he stopped now, like the air ate the words out of his mouth. I looked at him. He looked into the fog ahead.

"Anyway," he said.

I followed Cook's eyes, and peered through the whiteness to see a shadow, gray on gray in the outline of a man. As my eyes made shapes I saw the wireframe of Alphonse Ambrose, his tophat removing all doubt. I couldn't see his face, but I imagined him seeing through me, on the shore of some great river, flat eyes glittering with intent. It made me shudder, and I almost took a step toward him just to make him real.

Two more figures crawled out of the mist, one rotund, one worn and limping. They stepped to Ambrose, held out hands. Ambrose looked at something he was given, and made a cry eaten up by fog. Then he clapped the limping figure upside his head.

The figure took the blow, almost fell over, then stood again. The fat one made no move to help him.

Ambrose waved his hand and then turned away into the mist. The rotund figure turned too, and walked, and the limp man followed after.

The fat man had Lindsay Nelson's shape. The crawling heap of Frank Colt.

"How in hell they get ahead of us?" Cook said.

It was about then I realized my skin was itching fierce, pulling at me beneath my coat. I turned, grabbed Cook, and ran where I got told.

FORTY-FOUR.

The house where the old woman who ran the boardinghouse was being kept sat enclosed by forest, and Cook and I came up on it like thieves. Cook had found the house the day before. It was an old clay ruin, but perhaps it was safe. I felt that avoiding Frank and Lindsay Nelson through that fog was necessary, though I wasn't sure exactly why.

There was a window cut into the outside wall and shutters open, and inside we saw what seemed to be nurses gathered around the old woman taken ill. Her frame was thin and gray, like what was in her was getting sucked out.

The townswomen around her washed her face and her arms, cooked, sat by. Etta was here too. I felt a jump in my chest at seeing her. Cook cackled at me, and shook his head halfway when I glared at him.

We rapped on the door, and one of the women answered. She looked us over and cast an eye into the fog. Etta called that we were all right to be let in.

"But none a'them others," the woman said, closing the door behind me. "I'm not dealin' with any more of them just want to talk to her about that house!"

"Oh dear lord, I know," said another woman, sitting plumply in a chair, knitting. "Isn't it terrible?"

"What're they thinkin'?" cried the first. "Think she can talk? Think she can open her eyes? Heaven's sakes!"

The woman knitting saw us. My ink was covered by the coat, but the two of us were still a mess, stubbled and unslept. The woman scanned us with her eyes while her head stayed put. Her mouth kept moving as she stitched, countin' rows.

"What do you boys do?" she asked.

"I cook," said Cook.

"I'm in the show," I said.

She pursed her lips. "Long as you're not the lion tamer."

"Hush!" whispered another woman, worrying round the old lady's bed.

"She's right," said the woman who'd let us in. "My Lord, to let them lions roam around town! Well—there's nothing to be said. Nothing to be said." I could feel her eyes on me now, burning twin holes.

Etta was standing next to the old woman, staring at me.

"You're the only one of 'em any good," said the woman next to her. "I'm sorry, I know they're all your friends, but it's a travelin' pack of dogs, is what they are."

"Hush!" said the worrier, while the knitting woman laughed. "Bad enough we have bandits in these hills,"

"Bandits?" Cook said.

"Ayuh," she said. "They come with the fog. Can't trust these cloudy days." She stared through me.

"Don't listen to her," said the knitter. "You talk too much," she said.

"Do I," said the worrier.

"Well," I said, "It's good you ladies takin' care of your friend. I know we've caused you no end of trouble."

The women all stared me over.

Etta came toward me and grabbed my hand. She turned and said we'd be back, in a voice that put Cook in his place, and stopped him coming after.

She closed the door hard behind us, then shuttered the

window.

"Come," she said.

Then she took my arm, and we hauled off through the trees, sneaking glances back as we passed into more secluded places.

FORTY-FIVE.

There was a hill above the town, looking down into trees and thin roads and the sheen of mist encircling the woods. The hail was melting off, but the air stayed cool and the mist remained. Etta brought me here, one hand clamped on my arm as we made our way upward, stumbling over rocks and around the pine saplings as we reached the summit. Finally we stood at the hill's peak, past the last cluster of firs, among rocks and low grasses. Beyond the trees I could see the dark groove in the earth our small band had found on our way to the boardinghouse, years and years ago now.

And Etta lunged at me, her lips dry and frantic, her tongue in my mouth, but not warm, just desperate, as if she were lost in her own sea.

She slid her hand underneath my coat, crawling fingers skittering like spiders down to my jeans, undoing the button and squeezing, mashing her face against mine as if to break the bones. Half unbuckled, she dragged me up the hill and over it. She wriggled out of her jeans like a fish and I fell on her.

When we were done we lay there, looking at the sky as bits of blue cut through the clouds. The air felt warmer, like the morning had been a season. And we breathed together, chests rising and falling, mine old and scarred, hers tight and soft in that moment after.

She rolled toward me. I looked at her.

"I been sleepin' with the snake woman," I said.

She slid over next to me.

"Is fine."

And we lay there, and I don't know if it was. I don't know if that was true.

FORTY-SIX.

Etta was smoking, which she didn't do often, hunched like a troll as she looked down into town. Anxiety claimed her right after we'd finished, and she'd covered up in my coat. I lit myself and lay back watching her, waiting for whatever it was. The sex had calmed me. I'd told Etta about seeing Ambrose, Nelson and Frank in the morning mist. My tongue felt loose in my mouth, my body loose in the grass.

"You know," I said now. "I been feelin' queer since we got here. Since that storm the other night, things been all wrong."

Etta's shoulders shifted.

"What old woman said was true," she said. "The hills." She pointed at the treetops hanging around us in a patchwork. "There bandits here." And she watched the horizon, her hair and the smoke around her hair cast in light.

My skin went cool. "Oh?" I said.

Etta nodded. The cigarette had burned to the nub in her fingers.

"Oh yeah," she said. "All around."

Just then, all strange, a breeze blew. I swear as I stand I heard it whip up along one side and down below around the hill, in front of us and then back to its start, like someone stuck their thumb in a bowl of batter and wiped all the way round.

Etta looked at me.

"I worry for you," she said.

"Me too," I said.

"No," she said. She reached a hand toward me and tapped a finger. "I worry for you, here. You have troubles."

"Everyone's got troubles," I said. "You got 'em too."

"Not like you," she said. I paused. Somewhere in me, the eye opened.

"Etta," I said. "I know it's true. There's something in me, since I got here. I've got real bad feelings."

Etta nodded. She leaned back and looked up at the sky. "You can't see them, but stars are beautiful out here." She pointed at spots between clouds. "When night comes, north star there. And Scorpio, near horizon. You know by red star in his heart."

"I was only ever able to find Orion," I said. "My father showed me his belt."

"Scorpio and Orion, never in same sky," Etta said. "Scorpio killed Orion. You won't see his belt till winter."

"Never knew you knew stars," I said.

Etta turned to me and smiled. "You know me not so well."

"I'd know you better, if you wanted," I said. A question had been turning over in my mind awhile, and I decided to ask it now. "That first morning we were stranded, making beans outside the truck," I said. "You were tearing up something. Some journal, I think it was."

Etta's face was steady. "Oh?" she asked.

"Yeah," I said.

She stared at me then, and smiled.

"There are mornings when I look at you, and I feel…" Her tongue clicked as she looked for words. "I don't know. That I would like to give myself over." She paused. "And there are other mornings, where that seems quite foolish." She looked back at the sky.

I thought on that.

"So the morning with your journal," I said. "Which kind of morning was it?"

Etta sat up and sighed. "Right question," she said. "Wrong time."

She stood then, and walked back down the hillside.

I lay there for a little while alone, feeling tired. My clothes hung like a snake's shed, and I got that old feeling of wanting to scrub the stains from my skin. I remembered the first nights after that letter from Maureen, unable to end their crawling.

The day was getting warm, the idea that it had been near winter that morning just a kind of joke. I picked a flower stalk to chew, then put my hands behind my head to feel the sun on the back of my arms.

I knew today that the circus folk would organize and spread themselves all over town to find scraps of what we'd lost. They'd rummage backyards and vacant lots, looking for junk to refit for the midway. Setting up a show was the old magic, kicking in.

As I lay there, I thought about how a rite was being formed in these fields and back marshes. We circus folk practiced parlor tricks while standing at the edge of a wicked heaviness. But shadows grew higher on the cave walls, and this town no longer felt like just a place. If we failed we might be left to die here in this abandoned country, on dirt roads of bone and dust.

I slept and woke and slept and stayed up on the hill till afternoon. It was only when I could see the light change as it hit the grass that I made my way out. The hail and mist were entirely gone, leaving just the lonely pink late summer to light my way.

I walked through the harvested field where I'd made out Ambrose, Frank and Lindsay's shapes in the fog that morning, and now saw the frame of an old barn here. The shingles on its roof were stripped so that only beams remained above its walls, splayed like fingers. I imagined a hand and arm connected, outstretched and buried underneath me.

I saw stacks of wood placed next to the decaying barn in

neat piles, bound with rope ties I recognized. The teamsters had been here, taking apart the barn in pieces. Pulling the town apart to entertain it, giving them a show they never wanted. I wondered how I'd reached this meadow, what I should do with those neat piles.

As I made my way the night sounds warned me. Animals ran to their burrows to be with their families. Meanwhile I was led by symbols instead of reason, lost in cyphers.

FORTY-SEVEN.

I entered through the back of the house as dark set in. The downstairs was black but I heard rumblings from the upper floors. The crew was antsy. Night games were underway. A single light stabbed from the kitchen, and I wondered if Cook had been as good on dinner as he had for breakfast. I opened the door and ambled through.

Frank Colt sat alone at the counter. He was staring into his hands, peeling a callus from his fingers. A small pile of white dead skin sat near. He didn't look up as I entered. I could smell something good hanging in the air. I watched Frank with one eye, and headed to the refrigerators parked on the side wall. Inside I found spaghetti—pasta in one pot, sauce in another. I pulled them out, stumbled round in the semi-dark for bowl, fork, spoon.

Frank didn't move.

I sat down across from him, twisting noodles. I thought of him with Etta over the space of years, Frank finding her in some European carnival and asking her to ride with him, growing fond then bored of her, getting lost in troubles.

"Hello, Frank," I said. The spaghetti tasted good.

He looked up. He wasn't drunk, but he was gone in there. I'd seen a lot of men with that look, and I ain't seen one come back. Aside from me.

"Sue," he said.

And he disappeared again, looking back into his hands.

"You all right, Frank?" I asked.

Frank looked at me again. His pupils rolled back into his head, then forward. "Oh," he said. "No. I don't think so." And he looked back into his hands again, and he laughed.

"Where you been all day?" he asked, not moving. "Got real busy, setting up the show. Could have used you."

"Sorry Frank, I—"

"Show goes up tomorrow, Sue," he said, searching his hands to search for scabs, as if to read what he saw in the lines there. He looked up, eyes milky. "Did I tell you that?"

"Yeah," I said. "Yeah, I know."

"Right," he answered. "You know what you'll be doin'?"

"Why don't we talk tomorrow," I said to him.

"Right," he said again. Then back to his hands. His eyes rolled up, then down with some kind of dim knowing, skin hanging off his teeth. I saw all the pieces of his face, eyes floating in their sockets, bones under cheeks, each piece inside the meat of him.

"Maybe," he said, "If you can't find me, just ask Etta for a rundown of what I planned for you."

And he grinned. I used the coldness to keep my features frozen.

"That's fine," I said. "Won't you be there?"

Frank cocked his head at the ceiling, then rolled it back at me. He put his hand to his mouth, and pushed a cracked walnut through his lips. There was a spot of blood in his palm, and another on the counter. Walnut shells were scattered across the floor.

"I'll be around," he said. "But I figure you and Etta can help the others find their way."

I lowered my arms. "Listen, Frank—"

There was a cup of wine next to Frank, and he threw his head back, pouring it down his throat, then put the cup down and wiped his arms across his mouth, staring across the table.

"Yeah, Sue?" he said. "What you got to say?"

I looked at him. His eyes were glass, and swam. "Frank, I saw what happened to you this morning," I said.

The pieces behind his skin lost cohesion.

"What?" he said.

"Out in the fog. I saw you, Frank." I leaned in. "You an' that Nelson fella and Ambrose. I saw 'em whale on you in the fields."

Frank's eyes hung on me like bees.

"I mean, unless I didn't see it. But if you got yourself into somethin'. . ." I said. "Hell, I don't know. But if you did—"

Frank's nostrils curled.

"If you did, shit," he said. "You ain't got nothin' you could offer me."

And he leaned forward, the light on his brow and shadow beneath. His eyes were coal above his cheeks, and diamond glittered in that shadow.

"And I," he said, "Ain't got nothing I can offer you."

He sat back.

"I don't think I know what we're talkin' about, Frank," I said.

He watched me one last time.

"Yeah," he said. "You sure don't."

I sat with Frank however long, till the night crept in and buzzed my ears. Then I stood. He didn't move. I left him looking at his hands under the kitchen lamps.

Tiredness hit me as I climbed the stairs. It crawled over the top of my skull, hanging off me like a weight. I felt like if I pitched my head the whole of me would fall back down the stairwell. I held myself still and centered, so as not to rock and crash.

FORTY-EIGHT.
There was bedlam in the upper rooms. As I rounded the stairs, two forms ran past me, glowing amber—Simple Tom and Simple Ben, chasing one another under sheets lit by flashlights. They thumped the floor and ran off laughing into some dark corner.

When showpeople don't have enough attention, they start putting shows just for themselves—the need for being eyeballed bleeds out sideways when it ain't fed. You get a bunch of drunk carnies together long enough, sooner or later you gonna get some kinda put-on you'll regret. I heard a violin, and drumming deep. Laughter echoed and a warm redness swam beneath a doorframe, pouring like wet mud across the floorboards. Voices muttered and sang.

I passed the red room, swearing I just didn't care, needing to sleep. I walked to the little room where'd I'd been holing up, thinking Serry might be lying there, her hair an auburn halo on the mattress.

But I found an empty room, cool, crossed with a stab of yellow light. I closed the door and lay down, looking at the ceiling.

Sounds came amplified through the walls, so I heard each laugh and rise and fall of conversation. The energy had set the house awake. I closed my eyes awhile until I heard them bring up something heavy from downstairs. They slammed it on the floor, and proceeded with the clink of bottles.

I stretched and left my room, walking back the way I came. As I went, I looked in one of the rooms across—I saw a vanity, thick with grime, but with a mirror and small stool. And I saw Etta there, a ghost-image, doing her hair with her elbows up, back arched, one long curve from head to toe. I watched and a smile slid up in me, until Etta turned and looked, smiled back, and disappeared.

I began to feel then that this strange week south of Pickinpaw was a sort of ending, but what was ending I wasn't sure, and what had changed I didn't know. Behind me was a shout, the smell of wine. Both beckoned. I turned and left that place.

FORTY-NINE.
Wolf ears, wolf eyes. Down the hall some kind of masquerade was taking place, played out between reds and oranges hung all round. It was a big room, and abandoned, strewn with furniture and storage boxes. I saw a rocking horse and an extra bed outfitted with a canopy, chairs and desks and hutches and dry sinks. Lamps had been set up around these relics and blankets draped overtop, making tents and arcades and midways.

A firebreather, the poodle—lady and Cook were setting up to be the stars in a makeshift play, while Tillinger poured from bottles of cheap wine. More empty bottles near the door told me this evening had been going on a time.

The firebreather found masks amongst our leftovers and passed them out. The poodle—lady wore a peacock's crest, the firebreather a jester's hat and Cook was left in a wolf mask and matted mittens meant as paws. Their story seemed unplanned, but pulled laughter from the floor as others chatted, dozed or wrapped themselves in one another backward.

Omar and Mei Shen cuddled half asleep with lazy eyes. Serry and other dwarfs laughed loud and nasty. Etta was here too, red-cheeked, dancing with the firebreather, stage costume clinging tight to her muscles. Any sense of uneasiness I'd seen in her that afrernoon seemed gone now, drunk away. A guitar was plucked and tom-toms drummed by folks I couldn't recognize—perhaps if I had, my senses would have sharpened.

"I was born 'tween heavy trees in a dark forest." The wolf's eyes were shadowed by his mask, his arms cloaked in fur. "I come hungry to eat up men. Women. All they babies." He smiled yellow teeth. Drunk laughter rose. I thought Cook alone had lost the sense of himself—his performance seemed less fabricated than the rest as he became the angry, muddled dog he maybe always was.

"Then a hunter come!" the wolf shouted. "He shot up the forest! He shot me up!" The firebreathing jester bounced in, carrying a child's bow. The jester twanged his bowstring, and his little arrow bounced off the wolf's pelt. More laughter.

Cook, balancing his wolf mask, reached to the floor and picked up the arrow, then stuck it under his arm and stood again as the arm went limp.

"I was hurt," he said. "But I'm tough. I'm gonna drink me some man-blood!"

The poodle—lady giggled from her chair, twirling a parasol. Cook leered over her. "Or better yet, some woman blood!" he shouted, and jumped. The poodle—lady careened backward, her alarm only half for show. She snapped her parasol shut and swung it across his face, not slow enough for how drunk Cook was. She caught his lip with one of the parasol's barbs and he went down, holding his face in his hands.

"Shit!" he shouted. The audience filled with guffaws. Cook pulled his hands from his mouth and they were bloody, Cook-juice bubbling between his lips. As the group fell over themselves he spit expletives, announced he was all right, and told everyone to go on and shut the hell up.

The tom-tom and the six-string kept playing, ignoring the confusion. And I looked, really looked this time, at the musicians in the corner.

It was a dwarf drumming, and a big ape pulling the strings. No one I knew from our show, but that was commonplace—

this had become a kind of public house for freaks.
The dwarf smiled at me. The ape nodded, thick and dumb.
The dwarf only had one hand.

FIFTY.

There are times when your body gets ahead of you—when you touch your hand to a lit stove and pull away before you know the heat. There are times when the mind races and pulls the body after.

And there are times, my love, when brain and muscles find a rhythm, and those times are fearsome—when all of you is throwing itself forward without talk between your different parts. Some decision's been made and the part of you ain't mind nor body, but something in between is left asking whys and wherefores.

This is what happened now, in the orange darkness of that room. I stepped forward without knowing, watching myself as I crossed to that dwarf and ape thing. My hand reached out.

The dwarf's good eye went big and the ape growled so that I only had time to raise an arm when he swung his six-string, six lines of wire digging through my flesh. The wood rebounded with a tong, and all the crowd gaped, Cook and poodle-lady and jester too.

A bay window was built into the back of the room. In a second the ape and dwarf were scrabbling at the lock and went through it, all feet and elbows as they fell.

I couldn't chase them into an alleyway to clear the air and

punish them. There was no alley and this wasn't Coney Island. The past became the present, laughing at me. I ran to the window, watched figures running into the wheat fields.

Behind me Cook was sitting up with blood running out his mouth.

"What in hell?" he said.

One of the other drunkards glowered.

"Bandits," he said.

Things began to glimmer and connect.

Papa Canelli stood in the bedroom doorway, wearing a greasy undershirt stained with sweat.

"What happened?" he said, to the room but also to only me.

"Sue went crazy and punched a dwarf," said someone.

"Sue ain't crazy," said someone else. "Musta had a reason."

"Bandits," someone said again.

"I tell you," said Papa. "There only trouble in this place."

Perhaps no one knew else knew what he meant. But I was a city of lights and each one burned.

More movement passed me. Serry's feet were flying out the room, down the stairs, thump thump thump.

I didn't know what I'd started. I followed after.

FIFTY-ONE.

As I describe it, it's as though time slowed, but that wasn't true. It was a stack of moments—Serry out the house, me after, not so concerned about what she followed so much as what I followed, some part of me I'd buried rising up and tearing through the vines, as though the dwarf and apeman had escaped my sunken memories into the space of that amber room. Serry and me chased the past, as if it might make clear the muddy banks of now.

Outside the night held silence like a breath, still containing the sounds of breaking glass and feet. We couldn't see shapes against the black, but I could feel the absence those two figments left.

We breathed. The night hung empty.

And then we saw a shadow. Serry gasped. She'd grabbed a flashlight and she flicked the switch.

A man sat across the road. His skin didn't lighten, though the grass behind him did. He had lines in him, like me, but darkened grooves, thin waves from head to foot on every piece of skin not clothed. I'd seen Maori scarring in my time at sea. This man was white, and as he smiled his teeth were gums. He lit a cigarette. The smoke ambled toward us.

And he blinked, his eyes reddened for an instant. Beyond

him now my eyes adjusted, and I saw light through the trees. The night sounds cleared, and I heard drums and voices across the field.

The etched man smiled again, stood and nodded to us, and walked back to the forest.

Serry and I breathed out together loud. I looked at her.

"Hell," she said. "For a minute I was back in Coney Island."

"Me too," I said. "Stayin' here's just got us spooked."

"You think it was them?" she asked. "What were their names? Picture, and— "

"It wasn't them," I said. "It wasn't them. Christ, it's just ghosts."

"Shit!" she said. "I thought it was just me feeling it. Seems like we're dying in this place."

"This circus got too damn big," said a voice from behind us. Me and Serry turned.

Cook was pacing out from the boardinghouse, across the grass toward us.

"The house can't hold 'em," he said. "More came today. Canelli told 'em to camp out here." He laughed. "Now the freaks is in the trees. At least they all made it here alive, I guess."

"Fuckin' hell," said a voice behind him.

Two dwarves stood by the door of the boardinghouse, but we heard their voices clear.

"Bandits," one said to the other. They turned to go, heads down.

"Bandits," said the other. Like a ritual. They walked inside.

"I wish someone would tell me what that means," I said.

"I don't," said Serry back. She walked past me.

"Ghosts," she said. "That's what it means."

Silent, heavy, the moon watched us.

FIFTY-TWO.

I feel now that my narrative has lost its pacing, much as we lost ourselves in those nights in bad country. Cook went inside, but Serry and I stood outside in the dark a long time after the dwarves had gone, watching bonfires through the trees. After the silence stretched, another shape joined us. Etta stood there, wrapped in a winter coat.

"Is cold," she said. "Is late." We went inside, upstairs.

Two of the stagehands had taped over the broken windows where we'd had our masquerade, and someone laid mattresses across the hardwood. Cook had fashioned a tent of bedsheets, and those of us still awake lay together underneath in a mix of hands and feet.

"Bebbies, bebbies," Cook said. "Ain't no one find us here."

He kept the candles burning over us as we slid into sleep. Outside through the window, the wilds called.

SATURDAY.
FIFTY-THREE.
I woke for the last time under the faded pink canopy. Light shone through the fabric and above us the ceiling leaked, a drip of water pattering the blanket above us, dark and red in thin rivulets. I watched the leak as I came to, letting the rust-brown leak scatter across the fabric hanging over me.

My back ached like it used to when I was young and had early wake-ups on tour. Around me was a small band of sleeping carnies, knocked out and wrapped in dirty blankets across the floor. A stray hand and foot poked out from underneath, like a basket of children.

I crawled out from under the tent. Past the broken windows the fields were encased in fog. It billowed up thick from the earth, and beyond it I saw black figures running through the woods. My eyes adjusted and the figures became more trees, wrapped in mist.

There was a rocking chair next to me and I sat in it and began to creak back and forth. I saw Etta's face beneath me in the blankets, asleep and calm.

I dozed off again by the window, and when I awoke the sunlight was brighter but not sharper. As I stood, a floorboard creaked and Etta woke. She sat up, blinking one eye to recognize who I was. I smiled at her. She blinked again.

I looked around on the floor for socks while she stood and went to the window. I found them and turned back to her, Etta thumped her finger on the glass. Looking at me, she thumped again.

Thump.

I stood next to her, looking down into the fog. I thought a moment on Adam and Eve in the garden, and wondered where Frank Colt had slept the night before.

The mists were clearing now, and across the road the trees were barren. What I had thought was a thicket of saplings was really just a hedgerow, and the fields past it were stamped and trodden. Across them was a map of tents, riggings, packing crates laid out like a picnic lunch. But the layout was in disarray—the wood was a scattered mess, piles of warped boards and stripped lumber. I could see pieces of the barn I'd passed the evening prior. The tents were folded and set to be hung, but sewn together wrong, a patchwork of tarps and canvas.

"What's all that?" I asked Etta. She shook her head.

"Yesterday," said Cook, from beneath the canopy. He rubbed his face, then stood, and stepped up beside us. "I was tellin' you. It was when you two was diddlin' up the mountain. That Ambrose brought all this in here. Had the teamsters tearing apart whatever abandoned wrecks they could find up in the hills. The freaks who showed up during the day helped flatten out the grounds."

"No one's diddlin'," I said. "Where's Frank, anyhow?"

"Maybe we ask him," Cook said, and nodded out the window.

Down on the lawn a figure approached through the mist. Alphonse Ambrose, on tall thin legs, tapping tent and wood and rope with a long cane, checking each piece was there.

As we looked down at him, he looked back up and smiled, tipping his hat to us.

There was a murmur that went around the upper rooms, as the carnies woke. My thoughts swirled and I had tunnel vision on Ambrose's frame, waiting.

FIFTY-FOUR.

We all walked out and saw Ambrose standing next to his mound of mottled lumber, waiting for us. As we crossed the road he shouted that we should gather round. It seemed carnies had been slept up in all corners of the boardinghouse and in camps across the road, and now numbered perhaps twenty or thirty on the lawn in the soft morning.

"It's been a long hard week, I know," Ambrose said, his hands outstretched. "For this town and for all of you. But now's the time to make it right. We got one evening to show these people a night of the finest amusements they're likely to see. Time to lift some spirits and even," he smiled thin, "make a little coin."

"Where's Frank?" Papa Canelli shouted from behind me.

"Frank Colt is securing the final conditions for your performance tonight," said Ambrose, and the words slid over his teeth without shape. "All I mean to do is get you set up. It ain't a big thing y'all ain't done a thousand times before."

"This don't feel right," whispered Canelli.

"You already said it, now hush up," I said. Beside me, Etta seemed present and aware.

Without looking at a list, Ambrose began calling out our names. Some I knew and some I didn't, and again I thought how in the four days south of Pickinpaw the nature of our group had changed. As Ambrose crewed up the sideshows and the tumblers and the clowns, I saw how the casts of our acts were reconfigured in tiny ways. We were jigsawed, just hands and legs and faces, pieces taken apart and put back new with switched details. It was as if we were a letter of some ancient alphabet, and that letter had been spoken in a foreign tongue. It was a weirdness that came from Ambrose himself, a stranger in our bed.

Papa Canelli continued whispering. "Frank Colt, Frank Colt should be here, where is our ringmaster? No one knows. Night of show he disappears, no one knows, no one's concerned, they should be, merda, merda," he sputtered, angered but resigned.

But Papa got called then. He walked over to Ambrose and Ambrose whispered in his ear, and then he walked off, maybe looking over his shoulder at me. Somewhere his wife and children waited for him to come to them and explain how they'd play their parts in Ambrose's traveling show.

The anxiety of the morning had worn into a numbness, as if everyone's features were blank masks. I could only see them in high contrast, full burn. But this feeling passed and sounds of construction and normalcy filtered in, and the blues seeped into the sky. I was standing alone on that lawn while around me carnies walked by with a renewed sense of purpose, a rhythm found in Ambrose's mix of dance and traveling show. The tents were creaking to life, rising from the ground like scarecrows, all hunkered shapes and looming wood.

I was pretty sure I was out of cigarettes again. As I worked over this idea a voice called out to me.

"Sue!" said Ambrose, stepping forward. "Did I forget you?"

"Did you?" I asked. "You tell me."

He threw an arm around me and leaned in.

"I must have," he said. "Let's figure out what to do with you." He smelled of herbs and smoke.

And he turned me round with one hand, the bones locked around the space where my shoulder met my neck. Together we looked at folks working and hauling, ignoring the way he had infected us.

"I know," Ambrose said. "Sue, let's have you go downtown. You get signs put up, invite people to the show."

"You sure?" I said. "I'm twice a better hauler than a hustler. Look, you got the Bearded Lady over there raisin' a tent. She's a good draw."

"She's fine, she's fine," Ambrose was saying. "Down into town, that's good for you. Take the Twins for me. Those halfwits need a babysitter. Someone strong like you to grab them."

"Well all right then," I said.

Ambrose patted my back. "You're tense, Sue," he said. "Don't be. This ain't nothing. Remember what I said about bein' too smart."

And he walked away, nodding to folks as he went. We knew our roles. All was left was for us to play it out.

FIFTY-FIVE.

We were hanging signs in town, me and the Simple Twins. Someone had found one tube of yellowed posters that had survived the storms, and we nailed them now in grids up and down the center of town—across the grocery store, the library, the town hall, each building a gray shadow in a village that was only just. The sun threatened to warm, but didn't promise, and I knew already the day would size up cold. As the morning mist burned off the bugs rose, and locusts sat thick on sidewalks, railings, stoops and walls. The strange hail the day before might have scared them off, but in their downtime they'd been busy. It seemed like twice as many took up half as little space.

The Twins giggled amongst themselves with identical mouths, on faces that moved like masks, waddling from signpost to storefront to glass door, ignoring gawking passersby—mostly folks getting breakfast at the diner down the street. Everyone seemed dressed plain, easy for early summer. Families mosied all around.

Alongside the Twins I felt like I'd been kicked back to the kitchens. It gave me time to think as I hammered flyers, dodging my thumbs. As I hammered, dark thoughts coiled and uncoiled in me. I was falling into old lines and patterns, walking through landscapes rough with deep spread. Truths were muttering. A sharpness swam on the air. I was reaching into back rooms, putting on my jungle eyes.

I'd just found a couple unbent squareheads and set them to the wall of the general store when I saw a youth was standing there in a white t-shirt and green patterned jeans. He was staring hard at the posters through thick plastic eyeglasses, skinny and focused.

I flashed for moment on old Dwyer, braying like a jackal as I'd got my first tattoo in a jungle camp, bespectacled and thin and angular. I thought of him shouting at that old man till we dragged him out of the shop, walking him home, calming him down, cheering him up. I thought of Dwyer, and how he talked in his sleep.

The boy's hair was cropped short around his head, and his cheekbones stubbled with their first straggling hairs.

"That's the circus, right?" he said, not looking at me. I looked back at the poster, which read CIRCUS in big red type.

"Pretty much," I said.

"You're staying at the boardinghouse up the hill, right?" the boy said. He still didn't look at me. Potato chips were stuck in the braces over his teeth.

"Uh, yeah," I said. "You looking for a room or something?"

"No," the boy said. "Just wanted to confirm." I saw in his hand he held a map, and on his back was a rucksack. As I watched him he reached into the sack, dug around inside it, and pulled out a canteen. Eyes never leaving the poster or looking at me, he took a long drink.

"So you're going to the circus?" I asked.

"I might," he said. "I'm looking for it, anyway. Be seeing you."

He stepped away from me and headed toward the road leading up the hill and out of town. He walked fast, his rucksack jangling with whatever was inside it, his stride sort of wiggly and innocent.

I thought of Dwyer, face half missing and staring at me through mud, arms connected to body no more, body full of guts no more, hung upside down from a tree and skinned a hundred miles into the jungle. I thought of finding his teeth in my clothes.

Afternoon crept shadows across the trees and leaves and ground. It was cool as the sun tapered off, and I held Dwyer's broken, thick-rimmed glasses in my hand. His hairs and skin were stuck between the shards of glass.

The streets in town were getting quieter as most folks headed inside for lunch. I looked off down the road and saw the Twin were getting up to no goodness—they'd found a mother and her children reading over our poster. Ben was poking a stick up the lady's dress and getting whacked for it by her purse, while Tom chased her children down the street.

I knew I was counted on to bring them homeward, and thought again on Ambrose. It felt like he was working hard to get rid of me while he raised the big top. I felt unsafe in coming back to him. The tattoos agreed, crawling over me with prickles of electricty.

I headed away from the Twins in the opposite direction, toward the tiny boxhouses that lead down the street toward the town's only bar. I found the thin grass-lined alleyway that led between the bungalows, stepping through leaves and bracken.

She came to the door quiet, the glow of a burning cigarette silhouetted through the screen.

"Knock knock," I said.

She smiled sideways. "Thought I told you not to follow me," she said.

I filled the other half of a grin. Together we made a chesire cat of false cheer. "Never trust a tattooed man," I said.

She sucked in smoke.

"Maybe. Come on, you're letting bugs in," she said.

I took her under the yellow light of the stinking trailer. She didn't fight. The sweat and the dust of the kitchen shadowed us. In the aftermath I lay with her on the pebbly carpet of her floor, sharing one cigarette. Strewn around us were dishes, bottles, newspapers and old magazines. She lay on her elbow while I stared at the water stains in the ceiling tile.

"Sorry I didn't straighten up," she said, making o-rings.

"I need a favor," I said.

"Thought you might," she said, and blew out smoke.

"I need you to drive some circus geeks back to our boardinghouse. You can take my truck."

"And then what?" she asked. "You expect me to walk back?"

"You keep the truck," I said. "I'll come for it."

She took a drag. "Tell you, that doesn't sound like much of a favor."

"Maybe I need it done real bad," I said.

"Even so," she said.

"So you'll do it?" I said.

She nodded. "Sure."

"That's half the trick," I said. "You also gotta round up the Twins. But they're easy to find. Just look for crying children."

On the floor one of the newspapers looked cleaner than the others. It was flipped open to the back, and stamped on it was a copy of the same rough print I'd been hanging all over town—our circus flyer, crude as they come.

She sat next to me.

"You see this?" she asked, and turned the paper to its front side. "Up by the boardinghouse, where you all are."

I wiped the dust from the page.

"You knew about this, din'cha?" she asked.

"Knew what?" I said.

"That storm that knocked y'all out in the first place," she said. "It was a meteor shower. Maybe y'all got took down by shooting stars. We've had all manner of people through the bar the last few days looking for meteors."

I thought of the unusual hiker I'd met outside the bar, and the scrawny kid who'd looked like Dwyer. "Huh," I said. In my hands the newsprint lay prostrate.

The night peepers were coming out and making a racket,

mosquitoes and mayflies humming round the trailer camp. They could not drown out the locusts, whose thrum sought to shake the trees. I left quiet out the woman's back screen door. She watched me go, jangling the keys to the circus pickup in her hand.

"Night," she called out. "Will I see you?"

"Sure," I said. "Just come around to the show."

She said something else, but it was lost in the trees. My thoughts were clouding over. Bugs buzzed my ears and I slapped at them, driving them away while nails dug deeper into the walls inside my head.

FIFTY-SEVEN.

I dipped below the hill that led up to the boardinghouse as the evening deepened, past town on the edge of the flat roads and cornfields. I walked in swaths of color—from the richening sky to the just-rained greens of the grass and the black late-day shadows of the trees and the pale brown-yellows of the road itself. I fell into the rustles of my own footsteps on gravel, and let the rest of what I felt breathe out. It was all lovely, and I felt out of step with time—a young boy in the Ozarks on a back road after dinner, daring to stay out past sundown with a winter chill rising, knocking cattails against tree trunks.

It was quite a walk to get out to the dirt road beneath the boardinghouse, to the wreckage where the storm had swept us some days prior. I made my way through maps of trees inside my head that led me through the undergrowth. As I walked my skull pulsed against the inside of my temples, heat and sweat making my head ache down my jaw and neck and between my shoulders. I'd forgotten just how alone we'd been out here, smoking wet cigarettes and waiting for storms to pass.

The path traced backward through the ruins picked over by the circus crews and bandits, or maybe both at once. I saw the general markings of horror like its own landscape. There was the cracked truck that had held the lions, there the bloody severed ropes hanging from the tree that hanged them. There the grooves in the dirt from the trucks that crashed here, and our own footprints following after.

And like a stain that giant thumbprint pressed in the earth, a weird dug-out hole that still, three days in, felt unworldly. It had begun to swarm with insects as the sun set. I stood over the pit and stared, and saw things crackling in it that I couldn't hold.

I had thought I would leave the midget truck with the woman in town and then come back here to salvage what was left—repair one of the vehicles somehow, even just far enough to make it to the highway. My instincts, my skin, was screaming at me to leave and I aimed to obey. I told myself Etta would be fine without me. The weathered bones of Ambrose's new circus hung eerie in my mind.

But the newspaper, the meteor storm it covered, clicked wrong with me. Something didn't fit. Here on the dirt road the evidence was all around me, and I couldn't make sense of it. I found broken glass under the twiney ropes where the lions hung. I smelled a bomb blast in the dirt pit. The ground glittered with glass and gravel, but in them I saw stomach staples and tooth fillings and bone pins and glass eyes shattered, like the blown-out MASH unit where I'd lost so many friends.

How had I missed all this carnage in the soil? What pattern etched itself into my skin?

A memory came unbidden. I am seven. I am in my father's truck. We are driving on a dirt road in the north mountain country. I am in the back with my sisters. Their names are Susan and Marjorie.

They are both blonde, one older than me and one younger, the older one freckles and glasses, the younger bubbles and light. We have a boar strung across the cab of the truck as we drive, its legs stuck into air and clouds, mouth hung open in a burp of filth. Blood streams out of it in a sunburst over the cab itself. Pap will hose down the Ford when we get home and unload the corpses.

The girls and me are watching over a giant dead buck riddled with buckshot. It drips blood too and the blood is in our shoes, our socks, soaked in between our toes. We smile at each other and hold on as Pap tears ass through the backroads.

Through the back window I can only see the curve of his jaw and cheek and ear and this is how I remember him, as the back of a darkened face. I have never loved my father so much, have never so much wanted to be him.

I can't remember my sisters except by distinguishing marks. I've lost them in my old age and wonder where they have gotten to, how I lost them.

The scene ends with a flicker of tape like a burned out film strip, and I am still standing in this clearing over the thumb-shaped hole in the earth. Below me in the pit are bloody ripped dresses.

The dresses faded and I stood alone in the clearing once again. The night sounds called. The locusts shook the branches above me.

I turned. Beyond the pit was the worst of it—the burned-out truck that had started the fire, that had scattered the rest of what had been here.

I made my way through the junk that hadn't been deemed good enough for carnies or for crows. Stepping around piles brought me closer to the burned-out truck, and when I got up closed I checked, for the first time, what the blast might tell me. Wolf eyes fed me from my spine. The locusts sang their thrumming song.

FIFTY-EIGHT.

The burned-out truck was hardly truck at all—just ash and soot, with a dim outline where a metal frame had once been. In my daze the day before, the ferocity of the fire that would have caused this damage seemed no stranger than anything else, in the aftermath of the storm. Now I quieted my mind and reconsidered.

I walked the perimeter of the strange thumbprint-pit, and called it what it was. A blast radius. I sifted the ash and burned remants of the truck, and named them too: the point of detonation.

And just like that, a few things became quickly clear.

It took a long walk for me to make it out to the campsite where we'd parked the freak truck to wait out the storm a few nights before. But my steps were quick, and my blood rose beneath my skin.

When I arrived, things looked much the same as when I'd left. The firepit was where Cook had cooked, but somehow it looked like only hours since someone'd left it. I smelled the thick musk of smoke, and almost felt a low heat from it. Past it were the trees where we'd torn a half-sign from our trailer and propped it up with a warning that we were leaving, and past that a pile of rubble splashed with circus paint we'd left behind, like an insect dried to a leafstem.

I made my way to Cook's firepit, and pushed my hand into the ash there. It sifted through my fingers until I found what I was looking for. I stuffed it in my pocket.

At the side of the camp, something glinted in the underbrush. Or maybe it didn't glint—perhaps I simply knew what would be there.

It was an old bicycle, chrome loaded down with rust, not twenty feet from where we'd camped. Not more than two feet from where I'd stepped when Etta and I had looked for the Simple Twins in the morning storm. My skin sang as I unearthed it from beneath the leaves. The bicycle was small and creaked at every movement, and the tires weren't much but a rubber skin. I got atop it and began to ride it back toward town.

Behind me insects hummed, working hard to be louder than the racket I was making. As I swooped down the hill I felt the first locust fly over me. The swarms were coming. I led them in.

FIFTY-NINE.

As I rode down to the boardinghouse night came on, dragged by insects. I felt bites on my back, saw clouds of bugs at the corners of my visions. Beyond them was some shape I could not place.

I came up over one last hill and the locusts flew past me, thumping me with their wings. One bounced off and got lodged in the bike's gears. Around me the air was blanketed with a fluttering mass.

In front of me the circus stood out from the darkness. The carnies had been busy during the daylight hours, and now the tents and sideshow booths were set up in an impossible architecture, their limbs crooked and broken.

I swooped down down the road, wheels skittering over loose dirt. Pebbles shot my flesh and I felt a little younger, and braver. The locusts screamed in my ears, but as I aimed toward the house I fell below their flyline. I looked up into a sheet of them flying kamikazi. On the horizon behind me they kept coming. They flew over me and headed toward town, devouring the surrounding fields. I braked and dropped the bike, running for the house.

I ran toward them with my arms sharp.

The porch glowed yellow like an oven. Frozen faces stood in

the windows—Etta's blue eyes and O-mouth wide as I chased up the front steps. As I threw myself at it the door fell open. Cook was holed up on the other side, one arm stretched to the doorknob, his teeth gritted as he tensed to avoid me. I tumbled in and threw the door shut.

The locusts hit the windows like a wall of nails and the whole house shook, beating wings bashing themselves to pulp. I was surrounded by carnies in the front room and we all hunkered at once. We watched one another as the noise found its frequency and never wavered. I looked around at the current company—Omar holding Mei Shen, the Simple Twins gibbering—and watched as realization set in.

Locusts? Papa Canelli shouted. *This from locusts?*

Slow we stood, on a boat without sea legs. We looked at each other. Serry pointed toward the back of the house. The hallway had a small door in it I hadn't seen before, and we filed down to the basement.

Downstairs we seemed to multiply. Carnies kept running from upper floors, and under a bare bulb I counted scores of folks I hadn't ever seem except on posters—Ling Sung and the Spinning Children, Big Eyed Wally the Freak, The Sasquatch Woman, and a hundred others all huddled in the dark.

Over our heads, there was thumping wood and breaking glass. Cook was staring at me, and Papa Canelli too, their mouths making shapes. Could little bugs break windows? How were they in the house?

Past them and to my left, Serry made a head-count, her long tanned fingers poking air at each one of the folk in turn. Then she looked at me and mouthed two words.

Where's Frank?

My jaw tensed up. Etta was standing beside me, so I looked at her square.

Where's Frank? Her face made no answer.

I grabbed her hard to follow, and made for the stairs. We crawled through carnies to get to the house above, refusing to let one of them go, my boys.

The first floor we'd just left already seemed a different place, infested now with locusts lighted on doorframes and hardwood. The windows were mostly still intact, but the fireplace was like an open mouth spitting black gunfire, and we brushed insects from our faces and crunched them with our feet. I ran ahead of Etta, calling one syllable—Frahhnk, Frahhhnk—although I knew there was no need. We ran to the upper floors.

There was a tingling in me now. I was filling with water, drowning in rooms.

Lights only flickered as I hit the switches, calling Frahnk. Here the insects swarmed, my wife and child and dead brothers staring at me in the gloom. The first door in the hall hung open and I saw the bedroom where we'd gathered the night before, the broken window that looked outside, letting more hordes in. Outside the wood was shattering, panels cracking under their weight.

More glass tinkled, and Etta reached into the bedroom to find the switch. The light turned on amber and neither of us we screamed, though both of us may have wanted to.

The horrors were on the window, and insects were collapsing in from outside onto the floorboards and the pile of pink blankets Cook had strung over us. The blankets were stained brown-red.

I remember thinking that morning that the roof had been leaking rain. I looked now to the ceiling, and saw another rust-red stain.

Then I was pedaling backward, assembling the map of the house and running through the upstairs, looking for a door. Etta was an extension of my arm, tied to me now.

The stairwell to the attic had doors on either end, and inside was dark, but a hole had broken through from upstairs. More of the outside was coming in. In the dark we beat them back with our hands, and our feet crunched in their corpses. Etta cowered and I held her, the inks taking the brunt of it, and we kept our heads down as we pushed up.

We fell together, skidded on slick and collapsed through the doorway as it splintered under our weight.

I slipped on something that used to be inside someone. I smelled a stink of rotting parts. A wet heat coming from the attic room itself.

Etta stood behind me and I know she knew it too. The floor was thick with something that wasn't water and wasn't clay.

Dim light glowed a soft blue through slitted shutters. The weird flutterings of the insects beat round. There was a hole in one of the windows, like a wound pouring shadows and crumbled bodies.

Etta held my arm. She felt stronger than I felt, a twist of muscle. I needed her to hold. Past the rooms in me was nothing. I skirted closer to edge of it, ready to collapse.

Etta and I were one, mouths meeting.

I flicked on the light.

SIXTY.

Frank Colt stared downward and outward, hanging by a noose. Drool and blood and bile dripped down his chest, across his lapel. A fountain of gore covered the wood floor beneath him, soaking through. I saw nothing to remind me of the man I knew. Most of him had gone some time ago, and this week had taken what was left.

Lindsay Nelson was sprawled out below Frank. His tongue lolled from his mouth and his neck was bent from the weight of his head. He lay in his underclothes, slumped over himself. A hunting-knife stuck halfway out the meat of his chest. One hand hung across the floorboards, in a blood pool mixed with piss and shit.

The floor was tacky with waste. I thought again of the droplets across our blanket-tent that morning. Some insanity had got to the two of them, and God had burned them out.

Beside me Etta screamed, or didn't, maybe it was each of us, shrill and thin. Around us on the floor were piles of locusts, some popped like eggs and seeping, limbs attached to wings and giant eyes. The stink of them filled the room.

As we stepped forward, the room imploded. The windows shattered and a swarm came toward us. Bugs filled my eyes and nose and mouth. I was dried leaves torn apart by wind.

I swandove backward in that little room and heard glass breaking. I was thrown out the attic window and twisted like a kite through the night air. The sky around me cleared but I was blind and boneless. I called out, drowning in meadows under a paper moon.

SIXTY-ONE.

The moon shone. The locusts beat around me. I smelled fresh soil.

The lights came up, and across the grasses I saw circus tents, standing pure and perfect across the road, waiting.

There was a glow from above, from the house windows. I looked up to see the Etta looking down on me fallen from the attic height. She was at the center of a pupil, around her veins and humors.

She was the eye, unblinking. It watched me. It would not let me go.

I knew then what happened when we played our drums and danced our dances. I walked us through the night sea. I had been given sight to the world beneath the world.

THE WEE HOURS.
SIXTY-TWO.

I remember my last tour when we were called to burn down an indigent village. It was end-of-times and boys were heading home, but the brass above wanted to leave their mark. They grabbed the greenest of us, the easiest of us, and set to learn us something.

We were each given a pair of torches and sent around the village encampment, told to run as sure and swift as we could to set the place on fire from the outside in. And we did it, not putting pieces together. What did we know? We were just boys. You can't blame us now.

The jungle was wet, muggy with ants and skeeters and dragonflies, and it took a while to start the fire. But the huts inside were all dry sticks and bark. When the trees began to smoke, the villagers came running.

We began to shoot them as they ran. We stood outside and kept our shots low, to avoid crossfire just as we were taught. A lot of them got kneecapped and lay there bleeding out, groaning and then crying and then screaming as the fire leapt and started to eat them into charcoal as they couldn't run away.

There may have been some part of me—some part that felt things I can't find, that since filled itself in—that cried out, and got tangled there, burning to the dirt. Maybe I was of the dirt, and meant to grovel in it, an insect mining soil, encased in dung.

What I know is that the fires of the burning village became one fire, all fires. The glow of their embers became a circle, became an eye. The night opened and swallowed me.

When I awoke it had been strapped into a medical chopper, flying toward a hospital. The back of my head was a glowing ache. I would learn later that I'd been knocked down by an angry native child, bashed across my skull with a blazing piece of wood. The doctor said I'd recover fine, but something felt wrong, even then.

It was soon after that my skin had begun to crawl. The crawling never quite went away.

I came now from the blackness of those times, standing in a wet-slick field with my arms like swords, looking across the field on the far side of the road from the boardinghouse. It was here that a circus had briefly been erected, but now each tent was torn to ground, collapsed around me like corpses. The entire field was full of burlap dead and dying.

One tent, the largest, was standing in the middle. A few of its ropes had been pulled, but not enough to take it down. I looked down to see my hands crisscrossed with rope burns, deep enough in some places to have been sliced open.

Rain had begun to come up in a slow patter, then stronger as though no one had noticed, multiplying itself as the sky opened. A glow of lights flickered from the boardinghouse. Carnies watched from their windows as the rain and wind churned.

And there was something in me, some hunger, as lightning boiled and I stood among what was left. Still the carnies stared and even from this distance I saw their eyes, all dinner plates and fear. I thought of Etta, alone in that house's tower, and I couldn't feel her. I realized I was shouting, screaming at the sky that watched me. The words fragmented, but I could not repeat them now in any order.

The rain abated, and the night went tired, and long I sat there, huddled, cold. The pain hung vast and I found myself in a quiet space.

Across the street the glow-lights dimmed. Show over, eyes closed.

There was a creak. Someone came to stand beside me on the wood. I looked up. Purple slacks, violet shoes.

"Well now," Ambrose said. "Thought I lost you."

I looked at him and tried to speak. He pulled a kerchieff from his shirt and wiped the spittle from my face.

"Sue," he said. "Walk awhile with me."

He grabbed me around behind the shoulders, and pulled me up. He walked us both across the grass, smashed brown and dead. He walked me to the last tent standing, pulling back the curtain, and pushed me in.

I walked beneath his arm and through the entrance, under the the canopy, and into the center ring.

"Here," he said, behind me, in my ear.

Gaslamps were hung inside, turned low. I was in a mosquito tent out in bad jungles. Youth clung to me like a sweat.

Ambrose led me across the inside of the tent, through spots of light. It was dawn, dusk, and afternoon, all three.

There was a card table right in the middle in the dirt floor, with two chairs set up either side. Ambrose walked around and sat in the chair opposite, then gestured to me. I sat down. Around us I saw dismal shapes of things, like the inside of an old oilskin salesman's wagon—jars and bottles, piles of books, a skeleton hung on clothes hangers. An oldtime hoodoo show.

Ambrose watched me.

"So," he said.

SIXTY-THREE.

I tried to speak and found I couldn't. I dripped rain and mucus. Outside the storm pat-patted against the canvas.

Ambrose leaned back. His eyes shone in the dark.

"Sue," his voice came. "Things have got real rotten."

I could only look back at him. He shook his head, took off his hat, and rested it on the table.

"I just spent an hour cutting down our ringmaster from the rafters, stepping around dead bugs a foot deep," Ambrose said. "I've got a crew gone batshit that won't come out of doors. I've got you all tightened up. Hell, Sue. I don't like you, but I thought you could at least stay docile. I told you, you think too much. Too smart, I said. Guess I was half right."

I waited. He looked at me, then at his hands.

"Feels like end times, Sue. Storms of locusts and fire. Enough to make a man think of tossing it all, I think," he said, and outside the rain darkened.

Beyond Ambrose, the tent flap opened, and Etta stood there, framed. She was soaked and a shawl clung to her. We both looked at her. She looked back at us.

"Don't hurt him," she said.

Ambrose's eyes goggled. "Hurt him with what?" he said.

"I say to him," she said, and looked at me. Ambrose looked

at me too.

"Oh," he said. I stared at him. "I think the fight's out of him," Ambrose said, and sighed. "What a mess." He pulled a pack of cigarettes from his pocket, put one in his mouth, and offered the pack to me.

I started to feel my fingers, and reached for a cigarette. He lit me. Etta pulled over a crate. Ambrose passed her a cigarette too. We sat in silence, smoking at each other. The rain pat-patted against the canvas.

"Police will come soon," Etta said.

"Come for what?" Ambrose said. "We're too far from anything. Bugs ate up half this town tonight. We won't hear from them till dawn."

He leaned back in his chair, blowing smoke. I coughed, hard, and spat something from inside me on the ground.

Outside, the sky arced. Around us, the tent began to warm. The heat from the lamps was doing its trick. For the first time in many days, I felt my head begin to clear.

"You know," I said. "I think that I'm not well."

Ambrose breathed out, and leaned on the table. He looked at me.

"Yeah," he said.

"Hush," said Etta. "Police will come," she said to Ambrose.

"Fine," he said. I looked at him, playing with his hands. The silence stretched.

"Frank's dead," I finally said.

Ambrose kept his eyes on me. Outside, the rain continued to patter.

"Yeah," he said.

"Lindsay too," I said.

Etta and Ambrose watched me.

I reached into my pocket and pulled out what I'd stashed there—first one, then another. I laid them on the table.

Ambrose and Etta both leaned forward.

"And what are those?" Ambrose said.

"Etta knows," I said. Ambrose looked at her.

Etta picked up the half-burned journal I'd fished out from the ashes of the truck. Her fingers crossed the scorched cluster of pages I'd picked out of the fire from our campsite. "Where you get these?" she said.

"You know," I said again. "Ain't no meteor hit us out in that field, nor lightning neither. I know what a blast smells like. Maybe the storm scattered us," I said. "But it was a man-made charge blew up that truck."

Silence claimed the tent again. Ambrose picked up the journal. I watched him flip through scrawled pages.

"Still haven't said what these are," he said.

"Etta was ripping up a book just like it, morning after the storm," I said, and tapped the crumpled mess on the table. "Here's what's left."

"And?" Ambrose said.

"They're Frank's journals," I said.

"Okay," Ambrose said. He threw the book back on the table. "I still don't follow," he said.

"Frank said someone was coming for him," I said. "He was more scared than I ever seen him." I looked at Etta and Ambrose. "I figure you two were in charge of taking over this circus from the start. Storm just helped you along. Maybe you even knew about the meteor shower coming through."

I looked at Etta. "You knowing stars so well."

Etta stared at me, cold and flat.

"And these journals," I said. "You sabotaged his circus. These are what was left."

Ambrose leaned back and sighed.

"So humor me, Sue," he said. "How'd Frank end up hanging in that attic? And Lindsay, did I kill him too?" He paused. "Let me tell you something about Frank Colt—"

"No," said Etta. We looked at her.

The rain was rising again. It ran down the inside folds of the burlap, thinning it. The lights from the boardinghouse across the street began to show through the fabric of the tent.

"I will tell you something about Frank Colt," Etta said. She dragged her cigarette, then crushed it on the table. "Frank Colt was an insane fool," she said. Her voice shook, then hardened.

"Not always," she said. "But very scared, he was." She swiped her hand across her chest. "Scared take him over."

I looked at Ambrose.

"I saw you," I said. "I saw you hit him in that field. You and Lindsay. You two had some kinda hold on him."

"Hold shit," Ambrose said. "Goddamn it, you're so busy bein' nuts you don't see a thing for what it is. Frank owed money on this sideshow. Same as every year. I just showed up to collect." He tapped his cigarette.

"Same as every year," he said again. "Just a damn businessman."

He stood, walked to the flap in the tent that looked outside. "I'm so tired of explaining myself to you people," he said. "Frank's been paying off a loan for this circus for years. But that's all. You think I'd come alone if it was more than that? Me?" Ambrose gestured to his own thin frame.

"Sue, I do work for fearsome people," he said. "But fearsome people don't do only fearsome things. Mostly they're the same as you, with longer teeth." Ambrose looked at Etta, pointing at me. "He's as bad as Frank ever was."

I licked my lips, ran my tongue along my teeth.

"Frank said things," said Etta to me. "Saw things. Said he wasn't safe."

"Safe from you," I spat at Ambrose. Ambrose rolled his eyes.

Etta's chin went to the side. "Frank saw things that were not there." She looked at me. "He had got sick inside. He tried to keep it in. But he could not."

The words slid through. I thought on the man I knew, then past it to think on the man I'd known. Frank frantic, unslept, unkempt, weeping. Drunk but not drunk always.

"He begin to hire people," Etta said. "Bad people. No good for circus. No good for him."

I thought on the giggling Tillinger. On Nick Owens' greasy smile, on bandits, on the strange carnies joining our crew. I thought on Serry too, and on freaks like ghosts.

"Frank was set on shitcanning his own circus, Sue," Ambrose said from somewhere. "We looked through what was left of those burned-out trucks the morning after the storm. You know what we found? Dynamite sticks. Like some cartoon. Had a truck loaded with 'em. Could have gone up anytime. Who knows what he woulda done. Of course you smelled a blast. Lucky he didn't send the county on fire."

The world, once partially revealed, began to expel itself. My head rocked back and forth like a capsizing boat. "The meteors," I said weakly, looking at Etta.

"You knew the stars so well," I said.

Her eyes softened, just a touch.

"Sometimes a person can just know," she said.

"Goddamn meteors!" Ambrose said. "Use your sense! Frank paid off the paper to cover things. Got that oldtime fuck Nelson to help him too. I heard 'em talking down the score the morning after them lions got hanged, Sue. They couldn't see me in the mist and they talked the whole thing out. Frank was already half-gone, and then I came up on them. That's when I knew."

Ambrose sighed. "Couldn't be bothered to pay off a damn circus," he said. "But he could pay off some hick sap to run a scam."

I rolled through one thing and then another.

"What about them lions," I said. "Who got 'em killed? Who strung 'em up? Why not just tranque 'em when they got found?"

"Frank hired bad people," Etta said. "Bad people to do bad things. Messes lead to messes," She said, and crossed her arms.

I thought on Serry being barely able to find the tranque guns. On Nick and Mutt and Jeff, slinking through the bogs beyond the boardinghouse, drunk and ashen.

Etta's face was hard. I saw the Russian in her now.

"I'd found out what was what, and threw Frank and Linsday

in that attic the night before, Sue," Ambrose said. "Alive," he added. "I told some t'others they was up there, that they needed to cool off till we got outta this shithole town. We didn't know they'd kill each other."

Etta nodded. I looked at Ambrose

"Why not just leave town?" I said. "Why set up another show?"

Ambrose sighed.

"I was foolish," he said. "I thought I could do the thing. That wasn't a lie. We needed that show."

"Even without the man who owns it," I said.

"Please," Etta said.

I looked to her then, and through her. I saw her face. The way she looked to want to crumble.

"Hell, Etta," I said. "If Frank was crazy, then what am I?"

Etta watched me.

"You are troubled," is all she said.

The rain pit-pat across the canvas.

Behind Ambrose I saw a wooden throne, with a wooden Indian sat on it. His arms and legs criss-crossed with glowing circles that sizzled in the dark.

I looked again at the two around the table.

"So what now?" I said. "You can tell the police what you want. But if they find Frank and Lindsay, they won't let you go. Not after everything else. They'll jail up half, send the rest packing. They'll see same as we do," I said. "You're past saving this show."

"We know," said Ambrose. He blew out smoke, and looked at me.

"We got one more thing," he said.

SIXTY-FOUR.
The house burned and the bodies burned. We stood outside, our shadows growing long.

I hadn't forgotten how a thing was done. How to sabotage a place and make it look like nothing—bad wiring in an old house in a rough storm during locust season. We got the carnies out. Only the corpses stayed.

As the fire rose the carnies split off in ten directions, over backroads as they could make it by whatever means they had, the bad ones and the good ones both. I watched as Omar and Mei Shen held each other, shirking darkness, piling into Cook's old pickup. I said goodbyes to some of them. Most I just let go.

Serry might have glanced over one shoulder. The freaks I'd thought were Puzzle and Mr. Shift just blended in.

There'd be too many gone for folks to track us. Too many without real names and faces in those times. Soon it was just Etta, and Ambrose, and me, sat off in the fields beyond the fire.

"You two won't need to stick around," Ambrose said. "The rest is something I can manage."

"Still looks like a question mark," I said. "All you burned was what was obvious."

Ambrose looked at me.

"Trust in fearsome people," he said.

Etta stood then. We looked at each other a long time.

"I ain't comin' with you," I finally said.

She nodded and leaned down and kissed my forehead, and a calm went through me. By the time I opened my eyes again, she was gone in the dark. A minute later I heard her truck under the crackle of the boardinghouse. Then nothing. She would find her way, I knew.

"You better get gone, nutjob," Ambrose said. "More you stay, more I'll find a way to pin this all on you."

I looked at the fire, and saw every fire in it. All of me was drained.

"Maybe that'd be better anyways," I said.

Ambrose shook his head, and laughed low.

"There ain't no one here to save, Sue. This here's a thing that sorts itself."

I turned, my limbs clay, my body one thick wall of gloom. Ambrose stood in front of me and smiled.

"Sue," he said. "I'll tell you something it took years for me to know."

He reached for me, and with clever fingers found for a hidden fold underneath my neck. I swore in all my years I'd never known that it was there. But he unhitched it, and I felt somethin' peel away. Lookin down, I saw white ribs poked from beneath my breast; I saw him lift my skin and muscles off like a cloak.

"There's a buncha shit you done," he said. "That every man has done. An' those things ain't wrong or right an' you can't fix them. They ain't ever gonna change or resolve or nothin' else. They just is. The same way you is."

And he pulled away and there I stood, only bones and teeth and eyes. No body held me up. Ambrose was holding up my skin. I watched him finger the bad ink, the tattoos that pulled at me.

"Was a fine tailor stitched you this suit," he said, and looked at me, and there was a hallway in his eyes.

"Get the fuck out of here, Sue," he said. "I ain't got room for you. There ain't no punishment suit to fit the harm you done."

And he sat down, and it was over. As I watched he drew backward, cast in shadows of the blaze of that old house. He grew small and smaller, as the darkness around him deepenend. And he, or I, were there till we were gone.

My arms were still my arms, my ink still sat there, stained on me. I felt them crawling quiet.

I decided I would begin to look for you.

I hoped to find you here.

SIXTY-FIVE.

I've realized now there is no story worth telling after that—I have thought on describing to you what that next morning light was like, or how cold I was in the days after.

I could tell you how I traveled, to provide you some small comfort, to put these constellations together in some way might please you. But what came next ain't strange or special.

I think, for a little while, that I was more myself than I am even now. But what's real ain't always what can be sustained. I remember sitting round one dim campfire, singing songs to you. That's when I knew no matter else that I should come to search for you.

But I tell you always, ask me no more questions of them dark times. I will always tell you different, using wilder ideas, till neither you nor I will know the tongues I speak in. Best to keep somewhere in the middle as the closest to what I can tell you true.

You sleep now, child. Know that I have come through much to find you. Know that I will be here when you wake. I can't promise you more, nor should I, in this silent shifting world. I have spent my whole life searching for this place to rest here.

Now let us sleep. Let us talk no more on these sad things, lest they live on in dreams of wheat and sorrow.

AFTERWORD.

This book owes its conception, firstly and in equal measure, to Adam Miller, Ray Bradbury, and to *Invasion from Outer Space*.

Adam and I will have known each other for almost a decade by the time this book is released. In that time we've collaborated on a variety of publishing projects, and brainstormed on many more. We first met when I still lived on the East Coast, but we stayed in touch even after I "had the nerve" to relocate to San Diego. Of course, after the move, the time difference meant that our best chance to catch up was in the early evenings/late evenings (depending on your coast), and as was our pattern, most of these conversations usually turned into spitballing sessions for new projects. Since most of our shared creative work has been on comic books, it was only natural that one night I pitched him a comic idea that we soon began to call "the circus book."

"The circus book" as I initially explained it didn't have much to it, and the title itself wasn't even all that accurate. What I was really interested in was just one character—a tattooed man. I had no tattoos myself, but I was fascinated with them. I didn't know exactly who my tattooed man was, but his inspiration was a mix of several such characters from Ray Bradbury's most well-known fiction—the troubled, mysterious loner from the eponymous *Illustrated Man*, and the more sinister and arcane Mr. Dark from *Something Wicked This Way Comes*. I was interested in the grey space between these two—someone who was vulnerable and haunted, but who was also well-acquainted with a sort of supernatural malevolence.

At the time, however, I felt that my first priority was to add more characters, and to flesh out the plot. For this, I wanted to borrow heavily—perhaps too heavily—from a newly-released board game called *Invasion from Outer Space*, in which players worked together as a band of vintage circus performers combating a bevy of pulpy-looking extraterrestrials.

Adam was excited about the idea, providing we could alter it enough so that we wouldn't get sued (and of course, very little of *Invasion* made the cut, except to plant the idea of a spooky meteor shower in my mind). Adam even suggested we get in contact with artist Ken Knudtsen to see if he'd be interested in drawing the comic. But for that, Adam said, we'd need a pitch, so he asked if I would write something. I said sure.

"Good," Adam said. "Hit me back tomorrow." And he hung up.

I called him the next morning. "I've written three thousand words of that circus thing since yesterday," I said. "But now I think I'm writing a novel."

Neither Adam nor I really knew what 'writing a novel' really meant, and his response was appropriately cautious. "Well, keep an eye on it and let me know," he said, and left me to it.

This was the summer before I was set to start attending an MFA program that had accepted me under the assumption that I'd use my time there to develop mixed-media hybrid texts—a phrase that can mean many things, but almost-positively does not mean "pulpy dark supernatural circus freak crime novel thing," which was the best explanation that I was able to give for CIRCUS+THE SKIN during much of its development. By the time my program began, I was absolutely down a rabbit hole: the icky narrator's voice, somewhere between Daniel Plainview in *There Will Be Blood* and Karl in *Sling Blade*, was in my head all the time now, and I wrote little pieces of the story almost every day during that first year of school.

My feelings about Sue changed drastically during the writing of that first draft, and I continue to change my mind about him almost any time I review the manuscript. When I began, I imagined him as a pretty classic noir antihero, rough around the edges yet ultimately well-meaning. But as time passed, I couldn't see past the problems he presented: his violence, his misogyny, his racist and near-sociopathic tendencies that weren't easily explained away by the tropes of noir. It seemed that I pulled the parts out of me that made him tick, I began to be more critical of those same parts. I began to think that maybe Sue had a more complicated backstory than I'd originally planned (or not planned), so I decided to flesh him out. That exploration ultimately informed the middle of this book (and forced me to get serious about my historical details all the way around).

And still, I was left with the basic problem that the hero of this novel that I'd sort of floundered into wasn't feeling heroic to me anymore. But maybe that was what it was supposed to be—I'd begun the rough draft shortly after turning 30, and my ideas about masculinity were shifting. My trouble was that it felt somehow cheap to change Sue, who'd really begun to cement himself in my mind. What was interesting about him was what had always been interesting—that long strange expanse between someone well-intentioned and someone genuinely unhinged. This, to me, is almost the definition of our culture's most popular brands of masculinity. I began to think that capturing the in-betweenness of Sue's character was the real job of the book—like catching a fly in amber.

Several years later, I sat in the office of my thesis committee chair, Michael Davidson. The finished manuscript lay between us. I explained to Michael that I ultimately saw the book as a sort of "guy's guy" adventure novel—but one that actively worked to challenge and disappoint the typical reader of those sorts of books.

Michael sat back in his chair and pursed his lips. "Well, if you're trying to write a book that disappoints the reader," he said, "You're certainly succeeding."

ACKNOWLEDGMENTS.

No book—and no disappointment, come to think of it—is born in a vacuum, and to that end, a number of people need to be acknowledged for their complicity in this endeavor. Adam Miller—and by extension, Ray Bradbury and the designers of Invasion of Outer Space—have already had their contributions noted. Adam, of these three you are the only one I will admit to directly stealing ideas from, because you (probably) won't sue me.

And by further extension, thanks to Ken Knudsten for (eventually, reluctantly) drawing some amazing images of Sue and Alphonse that got my brain cooking. And thanks to those early Tumblr readers who gave me notes of encouragement on the first few chapters.

Thanks to the peers and professors who were my first real readers: Brooklyn's infamous Righting Klub; Anna Joy Springer (who, I think, politely hated it); independent-study-buddies Kiik AK, Amanda Martin-Sandino, Sophia Thompson, and Rachel Lee Taylor (who all liked it enough to push through the messiest parts); and especially to Hanna Tawater, who used to like it, likes it less since I cut her favorite bits, but married me anyway.

Thanks to the rest of the MFA cohort as well, and

to our cohort-member-by-proxy Eunsong Kim, who read the earliest draft of the Mei Shen section and warned me that the story I thought I was writing wasn't the story I was really writing.

Thanks to Michael Davidson and the rest of my thesis committee—Liz Losh, K. Wayne Yang, Cristina Rivera-Garza, and Ben Doller. I don't really know what any of you thought during that weird morning of sitting in an empty lecture hall, eating too many cookies and listening to my deep-dive presentation on the history of circus narratives as represented in such classics as The Circus of Dr. Lao and Freaks, but you gave me excellent notes and you let me graduate, so I'll take it as a double-win.

Thanks to Sophia Starmack, best friend 4-evs, for her thoughtful and critical response to the book once I began revising again; to Matt E. Lewis for his support and excitement in reading that revision; to Zack Wentz for his copious and inspiring feedback that caused me to basically burn down and rebuild the entire thing; and to Kathy Brannock and Ryan Bradford, who read the final version and reinforced both my own enthusiasm, and my own unease, over this project that has never completely stopped giving me the creepy-crawls.

Thanks to Laura E. Davis, Peter Kusnic, and Allie Wist for publishing an excerpt before the book was ever completed, and to Zack Wentz (again) for publishing another excerpt once it was. Thanks to the So Say We All literary arts group for letting me perform some of the work aloud while I was still trying to figure out what it was I wanted to say, and especially to Stacy Dyson, who told me that Sue shouldn't sound like he was "bringing truth down the mountain." Thanks to Ben Segal, Jim Ruland, Juliet Escoria, Jennifer Breukelaar, and Adrian Van Young for talking me out of the doldrums when life became a long dark tunnel of rejection letters.

And a big whopping thanks, of course, to George Cotronis, for finally agreeing to take a chance on the whole damn thing.

My mother and I can't agree on which circus paper set, circus stamp collection, or circus-themed wooden toys first sparked my interest in vintage circuses. Either way, my parents certainly deserve some credit for the way circuses have percolated in my brain, and throughout my work, for at least the past decade.

Thanks to those of you I've forgotten. When you remind me, I will owe you a beer.

And thanks, of course-of course, to you for reading...whether you're disappointed, creep-crawled, or otherwise.

About the Author

KEITH McCLEARY is a writer and graphic designer from New York, currently living in Southern California. He is the author of several graphic novels, as well as assorted prose, poetry, and digital media. Keith holds an MFA in Creative Writing from UC San Diego, and a BFA in Film from NYU. He teaches and writes about comics, composition, and multimedia.

Made in the USA
San Bernardino, CA
12 January 2019